Secrets and Surprises

ANNIE SEATON

Duckinwilla Days: Book 2

Heartwarming and compelling tales of love, self-discovery, and second chances in the heart of rural Australia.

The Johnson family

Grandmère and Papa: Margot and Robert Johnson

The parents: Hugo and Ellen Johnson

The Johnson siblings:

Charlotte Johnson - Book 1 - *Coming Home*

Julien Johnson -Book 2 - *Secrets and Surprises*

Oliver Johnson - Book 3 - *Wishes and Whispers*

Amelia Johnson - Book 4 - *New Beginnings*

Guy Johnson - Book 5 - *Chasing Dreams*

Lisette Johnson - Book 6 - *Together at Last*

Chapter 1

Sydney

The late afternoon sun cast long shadows across Sydney's steel and glass towers, doing nothing to warm the chill that had settled in Julien Johnson's chest. His hands trembled as he stood by the floor-to-ceiling window outside Emily's apartment, waiting for her to emerge. She'd refused to let him inside, reluctantly agreeing to meet him in the bar next door instead. He'd never understood why she'd kept the lease on her apartment when they moved to Duckinwilla Creek; she sublet it to one of her friends from uni. Luckily for Emily, they'd moved out at the end of the uni year. Now, staring at the busy street below, so different from home, he wondered if Emily had known all along their relationship wasn't as solid as he'd believed.

'I'll meet you down there in half an hour,' she'd said through the door, her voice carrying an icy edge he'd never heard before Charlotte's disastrous farewell party: the night Dad had his heart attack, and Rowena made her false accusation.

But he decided to wait for her outside the apartment; maybe she had no intention of coming down to talk to him. As he leaned against the wall, his gaze kept returning to the three cardboard boxes labelled with his name in stark black marker sitting outside the door. Each box felt like another nail in the coffin of their relationship, telling him exactly how their talk was going to go. The boxes held the last of their shared belongings—their half-finished plans to make the flat above the Duckinwilla Creek General Store into a real home. Inside those boxes lay the cookbook they'd bought together at that little market in Newtown, the one where they'd planned meals they'd never get to share—the throw pillows Emily had chosen to brighten their couch, and the matching coffee mugs that would remind him of her every day. Each item was a piece of the future they'd imagined, now wrapped in newspaper and sealed away. She didn't want them, and she no longer wanted him in her life.

Emily was going to put the skids under him.

The thought made his stomach clench. He wiped his sweaty palms against his jeans, determined to fight tooth and nail to keep her. At least she'd agreed to talk; she'd hung up on his calls and ignored his messages after everything had imploded at Charlotte's farewell party.

Despite wanting to chase Emily as soon as she left, he'd succumbed to family pressure; he'd stayed at home for two weeks and waited until the specialist advised that Dad's surgery had been successful. Julien had no hesitation leaving the store in Charlotte's and Greg's inexperienced hands and drove through the night, his mind racing on the quiet highway from Duckinwilla Creek to Sydney. The endless hours of driving had given him too much time to think, and by the time he arrived in Sydney, he knew he'd been foolish.

In more ways than one. He hoped he could fix what he'd broken, but seeing those boxes—the last of their stuff they'd been about to move to their flat above the store—had shrivelled his hopes. When Emily refused to let him in, bile had risen in his throat.

The door opened with a soft click, and she stepped out. She looked beautiful and untouchable in her city clothes—so different from his Emily, who used to potter around their flat above the store in his old shirts, with flour on her nose from attempting Grandmère's recipes. This Emily's spine was ramrod straight, her face carefully blank, her eyebrows arching when she saw him waiting, but he caught the slight tremor in her hand as she adjusted her handbag strap.

'You might as well take those boxes down now.' Her voice was ice-cold, but he heard the hurt beneath it. 'It's all your stuff.'

'I'd rather talk to you first.' His voice cracked on the last word.

She shrugged and walked to the lift, stabbing at the down button with more force than necessary. Her back was rigid as she turned away from him, but he noticed how she crossed her arms tightly across her chest as if holding herself together.

The tension in the lift was excruciating as they descended from the fifteenth floor. Emily stood beside him, close enough to touch but somehow further away than she'd ever been. The sweet fragrance of her perfume—vanilla and jasmine—transported him back to their flat above the store, where she'd transformed a bland, colourless space into their heaven. Julien remembered coming up after long nights working at the pizza oven in the General Store and how the aroma of Emily's cooking would greet him. He'd find her curled up on their soft couch with a book, looking up with that smile that made his heart skip. The flat felt wrong without her there now, cold and empty as though someone had switched off the sun itself.

'Emily...' he began, but she clutched her bag tighter, angling herself away from him in the confined space. Her knuckles were white against the leather strap.

The lift doors opened with a cheerful, mocking ding that echoed in the tense silence between them.

The bar was quiet this early; the after-work crowd hadn't yet descended from their glass towers. Emily marched past empty tables to the bar itself, claiming a steel stool with decisive movements that showed her anger. When Julien hesitated, eyeing a more private table tucked away in a corner, she cut him off.

'We don't need privacy, Julien.' The fluorescent lights caught the shine in her eyes. 'And if anything upsets me, I'll talk to the barman. This is going to be quick. I don't know why you came all the way to Sydney.'

His heart sank at her tone, so different from the warm voice that used to greet customers at the store. 'What would you like to drink?' he asked.

'I'll get my own.'

'Emily,' he started, but she silenced him with a look that could freeze Sydney Harbour, turning away and ordering a white wine while he asked for soda water. Julien knew he needed to keep his head clear even though drowning his guilt in something stronger was tempting. The city sounds filtered through the windows—car horns, construction, the rush of life continuing around him while his world fell apart.

'Emily, sweetheart, please listen—'

'Don't.' Her voice was colder than he had ever heard it. 'Don't call me sweetheart. Don't pretend this is something it's not.' She took a sharp breath. 'Don't make me remember how things were before you ruined everything.'

'Rowena is lying,' he said, the words tasting like ash in his mouth. Each lie felt like another betrayal, but he couldn't stop. His fingers tapped nervously against his glass. 'I went to school with her. She's always been a user. Why the hell would I look at her when I had you?' His voice cracked. 'She is *not* having my child.'

Emily's green eyes met his, sharp with disappointment but swimming with unshed tears. 'That's what hurts the most, Julien—the lies. You keep lying to my face, even now. I saw you talking to her late one night behind the store. I wasn't supposed to be there, but I forgot my phone and came down.' She gave a bitter laugh. 'Guess that's what they call karma.'

Julien's hands shook slightly as he gripped his glass. 'Emily, it's not what you think—Rowena is not having my child. I love you. I'll do anything,' he heard the desperation in his voice and saw his hands shaking as he reached for her. 'I'll give up the store, move back to Sydney—'

'I don't want you in Sydney.' Emily's voice cracked like thin ice. 'I loved Duckinwilla Creek. I loved our life there. The community, the store, everything we were building together.' She brushed away a tear with an angry gesture. 'But I *won't* build a future on lies.'

The truth sat on the edge of his words, begging to be spoken. But fear held it back—fear of losing her completely. Each lie was another brick in the wall between them, but he couldn't say those words.

'Please,' he whispered, his voice rough with emotion. 'Come home with me, Em. Believe me.'

'Why should I?' Emily stood, gathering her bag. Her perfume wafted around him one last time. 'I'm not even disappointed about what happened anymore. I'm more disappointed that you're not man enough to tell me the truth.' She finally looked at him properly, her beautiful green eyes swimming with tears. 'You've broken my heart, Julien. It's going to take me a long time to get over this. Please don't call me or text me again. And take your boxes when you leave.'

He watched her walk away—out of the bar, out of his life. The sound of her heels on the hardwood floor hurt so much that the pain was physical. He sat there, head bowed, before reaching for her abandoned wine and downing it in one go.

'Not a good outcome, by the look of things, mate,' the barman said sympathetically, polishing a glass with practised movements. 'Want another drink, mate?'

'Yeah,' Julien replied, guilt and regret settling in his gut like lead. 'Beer. A schooner. Thanks.' The afternoon sun slanted through the windows, reminding him of similar golden light in their flat above the store.

As the after-work crowd began to arrive, filling the bar with the buzz of city life, Julien thought about their time together. He thought about Emily's laugh, the way she'd throw her head back when something really amused her, her eyes alight with love for him. He thought about their flat above the store, how she'd made it feel like home with her little touches: the herbs growing on the kitchen windowsill, the soft throws on the couch, the photos of them together that he couldn't bear to look at now.

But most of all, he thought about truth and lies and how he'd chosen wrongly every time. The beer wouldn't wash away his regrets, but he ordered another anyway. Maybe if he drank enough, he could forget the look in Emily's eyes when she walked away. But he knew he never would; he loved her too much.

The garish city lights began to flicker on outside the bar, so different from the star-filled sky of Duckinwilla Creek, and Julien Johnson sat alone in a Sydney bar, drowning regrets as bitter as the beer in his glass.

Chapter 2

The floorboards of the old farmhouse creaked beneath Amelia Johnson's bare feet as she stumbled from her bedroom early on Saturday morning. Dawn light filtered through the lace curtains—Grandmère's handiwork, yellowed with age but still elegant—casting delicate shadows on the walls. Her head felt stuffed with cotton wool after another restless night; worry about Dad had threaded through her dreams.

She'd stayed up until after midnight working on the farm accounts, knowing Dad would ask about them the moment he got home from the hospital. The numbers had swum before her eyes, but she'd pressed on, just as she always did. Someone had to do it, and it wouldn't be golden boy Julien, currently chasing his heart in Sydney, or Lisette with her perfectly manicured nails and convenient excuses.

The old hallway creaked its familiar song— every board a childhood memory. There, the loose one that had betrayed her sneaking out at sixteen.

Here, the dark patch where Guy had spilled Coke and blamed her. Each step was a timeline of the Johnson family history, written in worn timber and chipped paint.

'Really, Amelia?' Mum's voice sliced through the morning quiet before she even reached the kitchen.

Amelia rolled her eyes. *Here we go.*

'It's nearly seven. Lisette's been up since six helping me, and you're just rolling out of bed looking like that?'

Amelia squinted at the kitchen clock through sleep-heavy eyes: 6:50 a.m. She tugged self-consciously at Julien's old T-shirt, the hem almost touching her knees. Her dark curls—so like Grandmère's in the old photos at *Maison de Rêve*—stood up in wild directions, a stark contrast to Lisette's perfect chignon.

Her sister perched at the kitchen table like a fashion magazine come to life in coordinating pastel workout wear, sipping a kale smoothie. Her pristine lipstick hadn't left a mark on the glass. The morning sun caught the highlights in her expertly styled hair—*naturellement* blonde, as she liked to remind everyone, although Amelia remembered differently.

'Morning, *ma petite soeur*,' Lisette hummed, the French endearment rolling off her tongue with practised precision. Their grandmother would have winced at the affected accent—Grandmère's French was as rich and authentic as her cooking, not this pallid imitation.

'Morning.' Amelia sat and reached for the coffee pot. 'I was up late doing the farm accounts. Oli asked me to update the spreadsheets since they haven't had time.' The "they" encompassed the two of her brothers who worked on the farm and somehow always had more important things to do.

Her mother whisked the coffee pot away before Amelia's fingers could close around it. 'You don't have time for breakfast. Your father's coming home this afternoon, and this place is a disaster.' Ellen's hands trembled slightly as she clutched the pot. Amelia knew she was trying not to let her anxiety show and to cover it with criticism. 'You can help me clean the windows. Go and get changed.'

Amelia sat there for a moment and then pushed herself to her feet. Through the kitchen window, she watched her mother's silhouette move back and forth, attacking invisible dirt with the same intensity she'd always applied to raising her children. The morning air carried the sharp scent of Dettol.

Lisette rose from her chair with balletic grace, water bottle in hand. 'I've done my bit. I'm off to my Pilates class.' She paused in the doorway, a picture-perfect smile playing on her lips. 'Have fun, Cinderella.'

The childhood nickname stung more than it should have after all these years. Amelia turned to go and get dressed, her bare feet silent on the floorboards that had witnessed so many similar moments. The house smelled of cleaning products and anxiety, every surface reflecting her mother's need to control what she could when so much was beyond her reach.

The kitchen gleamed almost aggressively—copper pots hung in perfect alignment, each countertop stripped of its usual comfortable clutter and polished to a shine that would have impressed even Grandmère, who'd always said a clean house was next to godliness, but a loved house was heaven itself.

'I'll do the bedrooms, Mum,' Amelia called, hurrying through the living room before her mother could object. The space had already been transformed—Dad's old leather armchair positioned precisely to catch the morning light and overlooking the shed where the boys would be working. Fresh flowers—Lisette's artistic touch with Amelia's carefully tended blooms—filled Grandmère's crystal vase on the coffee table.

The farmhouse had grown like a family tree, branching out over three generations since Papa had built it for his bride. Since then, he had built two more houses for Grandmère, and now they were settled in a beautiful new home that reminded her of her beloved France. Charlotte and Greg were spending their weekends in their second house, *Maison de Rêve*. Everyone knew how much

Charlotte loved that house.

The original structure of the farmhouse had held the kitchen, living room, and two bedrooms on one floor. As Amelia made her way upstairs to the second floor—added when Mum and Dad's family expanded beyond the ground floor's capacity—the usual stair creaked under her feet, bringing memories flooding back.

That was the step where Guy had fallen and knocked out his front tooth, crying until Amelia had cuddled him. Julien had hidden her favourite doll in the gap behind the bottom step during his nasty phase, and where Charlotte had found it weeks later, dusty but intact. The upstairs hallway stretched before her, a gallery of family photographs lining the walls—mostly the boys' triumphs, she noted with a familiar pang. There she was in the corner, gap-toothed and awkward at seven, half-hidden behind Oliver's football victory.

Amelia worked methodically through the rooms, trying to lose herself in the rhythm of cleaning. The spare bedroom had been prepared for

Dad's return with the kind of attention to detail that would have made Grandmère proud—fresh linens crisp as new paper, his favourite books arranged just so, curtains drawn back to welcome the morning light.

By noon, when Lisette finally returned smelling of expensive perfume, the house sparkled. Every surface gleamed, and every window caught the light like diamonds. Mum stood in the kitchen, reviewing their work with the critical eye that had always seen Amelia's flaws more clearly than her efforts.

'The bathroom cabinet in the spare room is a mess,' she said, focusing on Amelia while adjusting a dish towel for the third time. The lines around Mum's mouth seemed deeper than ever, her hands betraying a slight tremor. 'And there's dust on the top of the refrigerator.'

'I just cleaned both of those,' Amelia protested, but her mother had already turned away, fussing with Lisette's flower arrangement.

'Leave it,' Lisette said, her voice carrying that particular tone of martyred patience that made

Amelia's teeth ache. 'I'll fix it later.'

Something snapped inside Amelia, and her temper took hold. She was over always being the one who was never good enough, of watching her brothers sail through life with Mum's approval, no matter what they did. She was sick of Lisette's perfect daughter act, and she was sick of being criticised—she was over it and wasn't going to put up with it for one more day.

'I'm going into town,' she announced, grabbing her car keys off the hook beside the back door. 'Now.' Neither her mother nor sister responded, but Mum's look of disapproval spoke volumes in the silence. 'I'll come back and see Dad later.'

The drive into town was like a breath of fresh air. The country road wound through sun-dappled cane fields waving in the stiff early afternoon breeze, past the old Miller place where Tommy Miller had given her that first awkward kiss behind the shed, around the bend where Julien had crashed Dad's truck and somehow emerged without a scratch or consequence—another golden boy miracle.

The family's General Store sat in the heart of town, the warm sandstone walls mellowed by time and weather. Hanging baskets spilled over with a riot of colour—Grandmere's contribution to Julien's store's transformation. Tourist season was in full swing; the street was clogged with rental cars sporting plates from all over Australia, and the footpath teemed with visitors clutching shopping bags and the new tourist guide that Julien had designed.

The original bell above the door jangled as she pushed inside. The air was rich with coffee, and the aroma of freshly baked cinnamon scrolls wrapped around her like Grandmère's embrace. Greg worked the elaborate espresso machine, his movements precise and graceful as he crafted elaborate coffees for a line of waiting customers. He caught her eye and winked, then gestured to indicate he'd have her usual ready in five. For a school teacher, he'd adapted to barista life with impressive speed when Julien had shot off to Sydney chasing Emily.

Charlotte emerged from behind a display of local honey, her face lighting up at the sight of her sister. The honey jars caught the light, amber and gold. 'Thank God,' she said, pulling Amelia into a quick hug that smelled of coffee and comfort. 'Save me from the locals. Mrs Henderson just spent twenty minutes explaining why our jam selection isn't authentic enough.'

The store had evolved under Julien's vision when Dad had gone back to the farm. Gone were the dusty shelves of practical farming supplies that had been their father's domain, replaced by artisanal foods, local crafts, and the coffee bar that had become the town's unofficial community centre. But touches of the past remained—the original pressed metal ceiling gleamed overhead like beaten silver, and the hardwood floors still creaked in exactly the same places they had when Amelia and her siblings played hide and seek between the aisles.

'I had to come to town. Mum's driving me crazy. A cleaning frenzy,' Amelia said, following Charlotte behind the counter. Greg appeared with her coffee—oat milk latte with an extra shot, decorated with a perfect foam heart that eased her emotional turmoil slightly.

'You look like you need this,' he said with the kind of understanding that made it clear why Charlotte had fallen for him, then turned back to the growing line of customers.

Charlotte leaned against the antique cabinet they used for gift wrapping these days—another of Grandmère's pieces given new life. 'So, Dad's still coming home today?'

'Yes, this afternoon. We've been cleaning all morning. Apparently, I still can't clean a mirror properly, but Lisette's flower arrangements are worthy of the Louvre.' The bitterness in her voice surprised even her. 'The boys haven't come out of the fields all morning. Not even for smoko.'

'Ah, so Mum's on the warpath.'

'Well and truly. I'm over it. I'm not taking it anymore. I'm sick of it, Charlie. I've had enough.'

'Grandmère always said Mum has impossible standards, but only for certain people.' Charlotte's voice was gentle. 'Remember how Grandmère used to sneak you cookies when Mum sent you to your room? She'd say, "The baby of the family should be spoiled, *pas vrai*?" And she handled Mum by equally spoiling all of us grandkids rotten and telling Mum off in rapid-fire French,' Charlotte laughed, and Amelia couldn't help smiling back. 'Poor Mum. No wonder she's cranky most of the time.'

'But it's been easy for you; you've always been Grandmère's favourite.'

Charlotte smiled, the expression so similar to Grandmère's that it squeezed Amelia's heart. 'We've always had a special relationship, but Grandmère doesn't have favourites. She just sees what each of us needs.'

'I'm thinking of moving out,' Amelia said.

Charlotte was quiet for a moment, watching Greg manage the afternoon rush with the same steady patience he brought to everything. 'Maybe it's time you did,' she said finally. 'You've been doing a lot, I've noticed. The boys never help, and Lisette's too precious to get her hands dirty, and

Mum . . . well, she's not going to change.'

'I feel guilty even thinking about it. With Dad coming home...' Amelia picked at a broken fingernail.

'They'll figure it out. Or they won't, and maybe that's not your problem anymore.' Charlotte squeezed her arm, her grip reassuring. 'You know what Grandmère will say.'

'"*Ma petite*, sometimes you have to break their hearts to save your own,"' Amelia quoted.

'Yep, you got it. Look, there's a queue at the counter,' Charlotte said, straightening up. 'I'll go and help. Take your coffee in the office if you can't find a table outside.'

Amelia wandered through the store, sipping her coffee. Outside, tourists photographed the building's historic façade, smiling at the blend of old and new that Julien had created. The morning's tension began to ease from her shoulders slightly. Maybe it was time for her to move from family expectations and habits and find her own way rather than being there for everyone else.

Charlotte waved to her, gesturing to a table where customers were leaving. Amelia walked over and sat, cradling her coffee. Charlotte joined her moments later with her own cup of coffee, inhaling the rising steam. She sat opposite Amelia and yawned.

'You look tired, Charlie.'

'I am. I need a break.' Her sister stretched her legs under the table. 'I thought teaching was a hard profession. Now, I have to soak my feet most nights!'

'I wonder how much longer you and Greg will be filling in,' Amelia wondered aloud. 'Have you heard from Julien in the last couple of days?'

Charlotte's face tightened, her usual cheerful expression slipping. 'Yes, I'm a bit worried about him, actually. He really doesn't sound like himself.'

'Has he talked to Emily?'

Charlotte shrugged, absently stirring her coffee until the foam heart dissolved into meaningless swirls. 'I don't know. He's keeping pretty close-lipped about everything.'

Amelia hesitated, then lowered her voice. 'Do you think . . . he and Rowena?'

The question hung between them as Charlotte glanced around to make sure no locals were within earshot, although in Duckinwilla Creek, walls had ears, and gossip travelled fast in this small town. The store had been Julien's responsibility since their father stepped back—this temporary arrangement with Charlotte managing things was supposed to be just that: temporary. But Julien's behaviour had been erratic over the past two weeks, and now he was in Sydney.

'It's a pretty big accusation if there's no truth in it,' Charlotte said finally, her voice equally quiet.

'I think Lisette knows something,' Amelia said, watching her sister's reaction carefully. 'Our family's complicated enough at the moment without adding scandal to the mix.'

Charlotte sighed and shrugged her shoulders with her palms upturned—a gesture so like Grandmère's that Amelia hid a smile. 'I'll give him a call again later. Maybe he'll actually answer this time.' She paused, then added, 'I just wish he'd talk to one of us properly.'

'What about Emily? Have you spoken to her?'

Charlotte shook her head, her expression troubled. 'I don't want to interfere and put pressure on her. I mean, none of us know what really happened. And really, it's not our business.'

'Maybe we should talk to her. She must be upset.'

'Maybe, maybe not. I thought she loved Julien, but she took off so quickly, I wonder if their relationship was strong.' Charlotte shook her head. 'I don't believe Rowena.'

Greg appeared with another coffee for Amelia. 'Thought you might need another shot before heading back to the farm.' The froth was decorated with an intricate leaf pattern that put the store's hanging baskets to shame. 'On the house,' he said. 'You looked like you could use a refill.'

'My hero,' Amelia smiled, and for the first time that day, she began to settle. Charlotte had always had that calming influence. 'I'll be buzzing, but your latte art is getting seriously impressive.'

Greg grinned, his eyes crinkling at the corners. 'I even surprise myself sometimes.'

Charlotte looked up at him with such love that a little bit of envy shot through Amelia.

'You're a man of hidden depths, *mon coeur*,' she teased, the French endearment flowing naturally without Lisette's affected polish.

Greg leaned down and kissed her softly. 'Come and help me at the counter for a while. Robin's about to take a break.'

'Don't rush. Take as long as you like,' Charlotte said as she stood to follow Greg.

Amelia watched them, happiness for her sister overcoming her envy. They made it look so easy—loving someone and being loved in return—no criticism, no impossible standards, just acceptance and warmth.

She took another sip of her perfect latte, enjoying the bittersweet coffee as her thoughts circled; she was responsible for her future.

Maybe it was time for more than just moving

out.

Maybe it was time to start looking for her version of what Charlotte and Greg had found—a love that felt like coming home to yourself.

She dug into her handbag, pulling out the romance novel that was in her bag.

A girl could dream.

Chapter 3

The General Store

'You're not listening to me, Charlie.' Julien's voice crackled through the phone, thick with something that wasn't just static. 'Emily didn't just leave that night. She looked at me like . . . like I was poison.'

Charlotte pressed her forehead against the glass door of the fridge, letting the cool glass ease her growing headache as she listened to her brother. The afternoon sun filtered through the front windows, the dust motes dancing as customers moved through the store and making the local honey glow like burnished bronze. The January heat had hit Duckinwilla Creek with a vengeance, and even the store's air conditioning units struggled to keep the temperature bearable. Tourists and local customers drifted in for the lunch break, their complaints about the heat and humidity mingling with hopeful murmurs about an afternoon storm from the thunderheads building to the east. Charlotte pressed the phone to her ear, glanced across, and a brief smile tilted her lips at Amelia, sitting demurely as she read her novel.

The store's air conditioning unit chose that moment to give up entirely, surrendering to the heat with a loud thump. She watched a bead of condensation race down the fridge's glass door.

'Then tell me what really happened, Julien,' she said, keeping her voice low—in Duckinwilla Creek, secrets didn't stay secrets for long. 'Tell me the truth because something's not adding up, Jules. Rowena's been—'

The sharp crack of a bottle hitting something hard cut through the line. 'Don't.' Julien's voice had gone dangerously quiet. 'Don't say her name. It makes me too angry. How can one person destroy two lives with stupid lies? Why won't Emily listen to me?'

The store's bell jangled as Mrs Henderson bustled in, her basket overflowing with garden vegetables—the scent of sun-warmed earth and the sweetness of freshly pulled carrots wafted through the store.

'Afternoon, love!' Mrs Henderson called out, making her way to the counter with what looked like half her garden's produce. 'Got some zucchini that'll make your eyes water. Thought you might want them for the store.'

'Just a tick, Mrs H!' Charlotte called out, then dropped her voice again. 'Julien, I can't advise you if I don't know the truth. What really happened? You can't stay in Sydney forever—Dad's home. Guy stopped by with him on their way back from the hospital, and Dad's asking questions. He wanted to know where you were and why Greg and I were in the store. Do you want to say hello to him? He's still here.'

'No. Not yet.'

'When are you coming back?' Charlotte tried to keep sympathy in her tone, even though she was frustrated by Julien's attitude.

'I can't come back yet.' The words fell like

stones. 'Not without Emily.'

Before Charlotte could respond, a commotion at the door drew her attention. Local CWA president Daphne Carmody and secretary Joyce Mason swept in like storm clouds, their footsteps like approaching thunder. Behind them, moving slower but with lips set in a straight line, came Mum, with Lisette hovering in the doorway.

'Got to go,' Charlotte whispered into the phone. 'But this isn't finished. I'll call you later.'

The silence told her Julien had already hung up anyway.

'Hugo. Why didn't you come straight home?' Mum stood with her hands on her hips.

'That's a fine welcome, love.' He reached out and took her hand. 'How did you know I was here?'

'Joyce rang me. She saw you get out of the ute, and she wanted to know if you were going to take the store over again.'

Amelia and Charlotte looked at each other, Amelia's lips twitching.

'No, that wouldn't be wise when I'm supposed

to be recuperating. Guy stopped to get some milk for the shed,' their father said. 'He had to go to the rural store too. He'll be back in a minute.'

'Amelia could have brought it home. She might as well make herself useful.' When Mum looked away and leaned down to kiss Dad's cheek, Amelia pulled a face at Charlotte. 'Come on, we'll get you home now. You can come in the station wagon with us. Lisette can drive; she's waiting at the door. You should have let me come and pick you up at the hospital.'

'Guy was a good help, and you have enough to do with an invalid coming home.' Dad stood and smiled at Amelia. 'I'll see you at home later, love.'

He stood and moved slowly and carefully between the aisles, each step measured. Charlotte held back tears. Dad's heart attack and the subsequent bypass surgery had aged him a decade in less than a month, turning his hair to silver and deepening the lines around his eyes, but he had lost that awful grey colour and finally had some colour back in his cheeks. Mum hovered nearby, her spine ramrod straight and shoulders tense beneath her crisply-ironed cotton blouse, her lips still pressed into such a thin line they'd almost disappeared. The tiny muscle at the corner of her jaw twitched with barely contained anxiety—a tell-tale sign Charlotte and her siblings had learned to watch for since childhood.

Before Dad reached the door, Daphne Carmody's voice cut through the morning air like a scythe. 'Did you hear about young Rowena?' Her eyes glittered with the peculiar joy of the bearer of bad news. 'Saw her at the medical centre this morning. Looking quite green around the gills, poor dear.'

The temperature in the store seemed to drop ten degrees despite the broken air conditioning. Charlotte saw her mother's hands clench together.

'Some people,' came Lisette's voice from the front door, sharp as broken glass, 'should mind their own business.'

'Lisette.' Their mother's warning came too late.

Amelia stood and moved closer to Charlotte, the

sisters presenting a united front as Lisette walked to the counter.

'What?' Lisette shook her head; her designer workout clothes were out of place with the groceries and local produce. 'Are we still pretending we don't know what's going on? That Julien hasn't—'

'That's enough, Lisette.' Their father's voice carried authority despite his weakened state. But Charlotte didn't miss how he gripped the counter's edge, his knuckles white with the effort of standing straight.

The door's bell jangled again, this time admitting Greg with young Tommy Fischer, both of them red-faced and panting. 'Sorry to interrupt,' Greg said, his teacher's instinct for tension making him step between Lisette and their father, 'but we've got a situation down at the creek. Fischer's cattle are breaking through the back fence of the store—'

'Of course they are,' Lisette cut in. 'Because why should anything in this family go right? First, Charlotte turns up, then Julien ruins everything with Emily, then Dad's heart attack, and now—'

'I said that's enough!' Their father's shout rattled the honey jars on their shelves. In the sudden silence that followed, they all heard his laboured breathing.

'Hugo.' Their mother's voice carried decades of practice at handling family drama. 'Come with me to the car *now*.'

But he waved her off, his face flushed darker. 'No. No more sitting down. No more tiptoeing around this.' He turned to face them all—customers included—one hand still braced against the counter. 'This stops now. The gossip. The secrets. All of it. I'm taking control as of this minute.'

Charlotte held her breath. The sun bored through the side window, turning the store into a greenhouse of trapped heat and rising tension. The air conditioning unit sputtered back to life with a wheeze, stirring the dust motes once again. Outside, a cockatoo screamed a raucous warning to its mates, and somewhere in the distance, a mob of galahs took flight, their wings catching the sun like pink lightning.

'Dad,' she started, but he cut her off.

'I know what's happening with Rowena.' The words fell into the silence like pebbles in a still pond. 'I know what Julien's supposed to have done. And I know why Emily left. Guy filled me in on the way home.'

Mrs Henderson's basket of vegetables hit the floor with a thud, scattering zucchini across the weathered floorboards. No one moved to pick them up.

'Hugo, please,' their mother whispered. 'Your heart—'

'My heart's been breaking watching this family tear itself apart for too long. We've sorted Charlotte's situation, and I will not let this gossip hurt our family any more. Lisette, go and wait in the car. And apologise to Mrs Carmody on your way out.'

Lisette scuttled to the door like a young child and mumbled a soft 'sorry' on her way past the CWA president. She stood at the door and waited.

'Ellen, help me outside, please.' Her father

straightened to his full height, and for a moment, Charlotte saw the man he'd been before she'd left for university—the man who'd built the store into what it was today while honouring everything Papa and Grandmère had created, the man whose reputation for fairness matched Papa's in every way. 'No more secrets. No more surprises,' he said as he walked to the door, holding Ellen's hand.

Charlotte looked around at her family—at Lisette's perfectly made-up face now showing cracks of genuine emotion, at their mother's barely hidden fear, at their father's determined stance that couldn't entirely hide his trembling hands.

And finally, at Greg, who'd chosen her and become a part of this messy, complicated family despite everything.

And she'd said she'd ring Julien back. Maybe she'd just forget about doing that as Dad had instructed.

Chapter 4

Charlotte's hands shook as she tried to fit the key into the lock at the bottom of the stairs leading to the flat above Duckinwilla Creek General Store. Throughout the week, she and Greg stayed here in the spare room and then spent the weekends at *Maison de Rêve*. She'd been holding it together since her family had left, leaving some curious customers behind. Alone now in the early evening, her composure was cracking.

She paused halfway up the steep wooden stairs, pressing her fingertips to her temples where a headache had been building since morning. Somewhere in her bag, her phone buzzed again. She ignored it; if it was Julien, he could wait this time.

The scent of garlic and herbs drifted down the stairwell: Greg had come upstairs while she rang off the till and was cooking dinner because he knew when she needed some TLC. He'd probably heard her dropping things and muttering to herself from downstairs as she'd locked up. Her shoulders, tight from the long day of work—not to mention family tension—relaxed slightly.

All day on her feet, Dad's health, Julien's situation—which she suspected was of his own doing, Amelia's unhappiness—Mum was so hard on her for no reason, and Lisette's bitchiness all overwhelmed her as she reached the top step, and she brushed a tear away.

When she pushed open the door, Greg held out her favourite mug, the chipped blue one Julien had salvaged from the store's stockroom during the renovations. He'd remembered it had been her favourite and put it aside. Her brother wasn't all bad; he'd just made some stupid decisions. For someone who ran the store so well, he couldn't do a thing right in his personal life.

Steam curled from the mug as she took it, and she inhaled. 'Chamomile tea. Thank you. You're a darling.'

'That bad?' he asked quietly.

Charlotte dropped her bag onto the sofa. 'You saw half of it. And yes, Dad lost his cool.'

Greg leaned against their kitchen counter, giving her space even as his eyes stayed steady on her face. 'And the rest? Because I know you too well, there's more.'

'Plus, Mum's barely speaking to anyone, but apparently, she can find the energy to tell me I need to "fix things" with Julien.' Charlotte's laugh came out bitter. 'Because clearly, I'm the only one who can convince him that camping outside his ex-girlfriend's house is not a healthy coping mechanism.'

'While also solving the mystery of the missing receipts, stopping Amelia from emptying her bank account on a one-way ticket to Japan, and probably bringing about world peace?' Greg's voice was gentle, but there was an edge there—protectiveness, she knew.

Charlotte opened and closed her fists, a nervous habit she'd developed in the weeks since they'd cancelled their France tickets to stay and help after Dad's heart attack.

Greg crossed to her then, but instead of hugging

her, he took her hands, stilling the anxious movement. 'Remember what you told me the day we decided to stay? That some things matter more than Paris in the spring?'

'I remember. I also remember we had actual tickets.' She met his eyes. 'Sometimes I wonder if we made the right choice. If any of the family would do the same for us.'

'They would. They're just—' Greg paused, choosing his words carefully— 'a bit lost right now. All of them. And they're looking to you because you're always calm, logical and settled.'

'And tired,' Charlotte whispered.

'I know, sweetheart.' Greg's thumb traced over her fingers. 'That's why you have me. To look out for you, as I know you would do for me.'

'I just don't know how to stop being the one they all lean on,' she admitted finally. 'I wish Guy and Oliver would step up sometimes.'

'Maybe you don't have to stop. Maybe you just have to learn to pull back occasionally.' Greg pulled her close, and she let herself sag against him, just for a moment. 'And maybe, when things settle, we book new tickets. France is still waiting.'

'With my luck, Amelia will probably be living in France before I get there,' Charlotte said, but there was a ghost of humour in her voice.

'Japan? France? Then we'll have a tour guide.' Greg pressed a kiss to her forehead. Something loosened in Charlotte's chest; not *all* the stress, but enough. Enough to face another day of being there for everyone. Enough to keep trying to guide her family back to solid ground. Enough to believe that France was still there, waiting.

'I do love you, Greg,' she said softly. 'Even when I'm terrible company.'

'Maybe we could go to France for our honeymoon?' he said against her cheek.

Charlotte pulled away and stared at him, one hand over her mouth. 'Um, is that a proposal?'

'Would you rather I got down on my knee?'

'Yes, yes, yes,' Charlotte cried, her voice breaking.

'On my knee?' Greg smiled at her.

'No, silly, that was yes, I'll marry you.'

Greg cupped her face in his hands, his thumbs brushing away the happy tears that had started falling. When his lips met hers, Charlotte tasted salt and sweetness and promise. It was a gentle kiss, tender and lingering, full of all the words they didn't need to say. When they finally pulled apart, Greg rested his forehead against hers, both of them sharing the same happy smile.

Her phone buzzed again. Family. Work. Responsibilities.

She ignored it.

Outside, the sun set over Duckinwilla Creek, the sky firing in golden and purple hues, bathing them in a soft light. Tomorrow would bring new family battles to fight and new problems to overcome. But right now, with Greg's love, her strength grew.

Charlotte's heart fluttered as she looked up at the man she loved, the evening light turning his dark eyes soft and warm. The familiar sounds of the street below faded away until all she could hear was the rhythm of their breathing.

'Let's make that our secret for a while?' she whispered, reaching up to trace his jawline with gentle fingers. 'Just ours.'

'Until all the family angst has passed?' Greg's smile was tender as he caught her hand in his, pressing a kiss to her palm. 'Although I might burst from happiness before then.'

'You know me well.' Charlotte's laugh was soft and full of joy as she rose on her tiptoes. Greg's arms slid around her waist, drawing her closer, and when their lips met, the kiss was gentle at first, then deeper, full of promise and shared dreams.

'I love you,' she murmured against his lips. 'Every wonderful, patient, understanding bit of you.'

'And I love you,' he whispered back. 'My beautiful, strong, amazing Charlotte.'

Chapter 5

Duckinwilla Creek - the next day

The heat was relentless for the third day in a row and pressed against the windows of Lucy Lou's Hair Salon like a thick blanket. The heat of the hair dryers running inside created fog on the glass, turning the main street of Duckinwilla Creek into a shimmering mirage. Inside, the air conditioning hummed a steady balance to the whir of hair dryers, keeping the small salon cool and inviting. Amelia sank into the familiar black leather chair, breathing in the mingled scents of hair products and Lucy's signature lemon candles. Lucy's salon and Jerry's barber shop next door had been fixtures in town since before Amelia was born, the cheerful yellow walls witnessing countless transformations, hearing many secrets, and inspiring fresh starts.

Her reflection stared back at her from the mirror—sensible Amelia Johnson, youngest daughter of the town's most talked-about family, wearing the same safe, practical hairstyle she'd had since the first year of high school. The wooden floor creaked beneath the chair as Lucy Lou adjusted its height, her collection of bangles jangling their familiar melody.

'Right then, love.' She draped the cape around Amelia's shoulders with the flourish of someone who understood that a hair appointment was as much for counselling as transformation. 'What're we doing today? The usual trim and highlights?' Her bright eyes met Amelia's in the mirror.

Amelia's fingers twisted in her lap beneath the cape. 'Actually, I want something different.' The words came out barely above a whisper, then stronger, 'Something wild.'

Lucy Lou's eyebrows shot up, her red and silver-streaked curls bouncing as she leaned in. 'Wild? You?' She lowered her voice conspiratorially. 'Now, this I have to hear about.'

In the background, the usual suspects—Mabel, Edna, and Doris—sat under their dryers like a Greek chorus, curlers in their hair as per their weekly ritual. Their magazines didn't entirely hide their interest. Amelia caught Mabel's reflection, pretending not to listen, and something inside her snapped.

'I'm just . . . over it, Lucy Lou.' The words felt like a confession. 'So tired of being the sensible one. The reliable one. The daughter who never causes trouble.' She met her own eyes in the mirror, seeing Grandmère's determination there. 'The one who keeps the peace and picks up the pieces and pretends everything's fine.'

The salon fell silent. Even the hair dryers seemed to pause as the hairdresser began sectioning Amelia's hair; her practised movements were gentle but sure. 'I hear your dad came home from hospital yesterday.' Her fingers worked through a knot with infinite care. 'He's doing well, isn't he?'

'Yes, thank God.' Amelia's throat tightened. 'But that's just one crisis sorted. Everyone in my family's gone mad. Properly mad.' The words tumbled out like water through a broken dam. 'Lisette and Charlotte are at war over the store accounts—as if spreadsheets matter more than being sisters. Julien's off in Sydney, making an absolute mess of his life with this Rowena business and breaking Emily's heart in the process. And the boys?' She gave a laugh that wasn't quite steady. 'Guy and Oliver are so buried in the farm, it's like they've forgotten how to have an actual conversation that isn't about cattle or cane or the new mango trees.'

'Sounds like you need more than just a haircut, love.' Lucy Lou reached for her collection of hair dyes, fingers hovering over the bright colours like an artist selecting paints. 'How about we start with some electric blue? Really give the old biddies something to talk about besides your family drama? It'll take a while because I'll have to bleach it first and then dry it so there's no moisture at all, and then I'll put the colours on.'

'Colours?'

'Yes, I think you need a rainbow.'

Amelia caught sight of the trio under the dryers, quickly hiding behind their magazines. 'Why not?

It's my day off from pre-school, and you know what? I'd rather sit in here all day than be at home.' The recklessness in her voice surprised her. 'They're already talking about me anyway. Did you know Lisette called me Cinderella yesterday? As if I'm the one choosing to stay home and help!' Her voice cracked slightly. 'I'm supposed to love my family, but sometimes . . . sometimes I don't even like them very much.'

'Did you ever think maybe that's normal?' Lucy mixed the bleach with deft rubber-gloved fingers, the pungent smell of chemicals mixing with the lemon candles. 'Loving family doesn't mean you have to love everything they do.'

'But that's just it—I feel guilty even thinking that way.' Amelia watched in the mirror as Lucy began applying the white paste. 'Sometimes I dream about just . . . leaving and going somewhere where nobody knows the Johnsons, where I don't have to be the sensible boring one, where I could just be . . . me. Whoever that is.'

'Where would you go?' Lucy's question held no

judgment, just genuine curiosity.

'Melbourne, maybe. Or overseas. I love the assistant work at the preschool, and the director said there's a traineeship coming up soon. I could get my qualifications, and having a pay packet now, I could maybe find a rental in town.'

'Good luck with that,' Lucy Lou said dryly. 'Since your brother's been president of the Chamber of Commerce, there are no rentals available. Everyone wants to live in Duckinwilla Creek now!'

'I could teach English in Japan. I've always wanted to go there. Live in a tiny apartment where no one expects me to cook family dinner or mediate arguments or pretend I don't see what's happening with Julien and Rowena.' She met Lucy's eyes in the mirror. 'Is that awful of me? To want to run away when Dad's just gotten home from hospital?'

'Of course not, darling.' Lucy's voice was gentle but firm. 'Sometimes you need to step away to find yourself. Look at me—I didn't always have red hair and own this salon, you know. I spent three years in Perth doing whatever took my fancy before

I came back here. The Creek'll always be here if you want to come back.'

From under the dryers, Mabel's voice carried clearly, 'Did you hear about Julien and that Rowena girl? I heard—'

Before Amelia could hear the latest gossip about her brother, Lucy Lou placed a roll of foil over her head, making her giggle. 'Now sit tight for forty-five minutes, and I'll get the three oldies done,' she said quietly.

'I heard that, Lucy Lou. I'm the same age as you,' Mabel yelled over the noise of the dryer. 'We started school the same day.'

'We'll have none of that today, thank you very much, Miss Mabel, who I *didn't* go to school with.' Lucy Lou rolled her eyes. 'You've got the wrong person, Mabel. You're getting forgetful.' She winked at Amelia before going over to the dryers, her sharp voice cutting through the gossip like a knife. 'This is a drama-free zone.'

Half an hour later, the three biddies had been permed, primped, and paid their bills.

Lucy Lou chuckled as they walked out. 'I charged them more today. It's about time I put my rates up. Now, come on over to the basin, and we'll get started.' Her eyes were kind as she reached for the orange dye. 'Now, how about we add some sunset red to go with that blue? Really give them something to talk about?'

'Do your worst.' Amelia settled back, feeling the tension lifting from her shoulders. 'At least this drama will be *my* choice.'

As Lucy Lou worked, transforming Amelia's sensible brown hair into a riot of colour, they talked about everything and nothing: Lucy's plans to expand the salon, the secret notebook of travel plans hidden under Amelia's bed, the way the town seemed to be shrinking around her lately.

'You know what the real problem is?' Amelia said as Lucy added the final touches of emerald green. 'Everyone's forgotten how to be happy. It's all business and drama and responsibilities. Even the boys used to be the life of every party, and now they're in bed by nine because they have to check the irrigation system at dawn. When did we all get so . . . old? We're not kids anymore.'

'Sounds like the Johnsons need a good shake-up,' Lucy said, stepping back to admire her work. 'Maybe your new look will start the trend. Sometimes, the smallest rebellions make the biggest waves.'

Amelia stared at her reflection, barely recognising the woman in the mirror with the striking blue, green, and red-orange hair. It should have looked ridiculous, but somehow it worked, like a tropical sunset captured in hair, like courage made visible. It reminded her of the paintings in Grandmère's parlour, all bold colours and courageous strokes, like those Cézanne paintings she'd studied in art class at high school.

'Oh, that'll give them something to talk about, all right.' She touched one of the blue streaks gently. 'I'm not sure what Grandmère will say, though.'

'You might be surprised.' Lucy's smile was knowing. 'That grandmother of yours wasn't always the proper lady she is now. Ask her about Paris sometime.'

'Don't tell me Grandmère shares her secrets with you?'

'My clients all know I'm like a confessional. What I hear stays here.'

Amelia giggled. 'You need a sign on the wall that says that.'

As Lucy Lou removed the cape, Amelia stood, feeling much better. Through the window, she could see the main street and all the usual activity.

'Thanks, Lucy.' She reached for her purse, but the words meant more than gratitude for a hair colour. 'For everything.'

'Any time, love.' Lucy winked. 'Now go on out there and show them what a Johnson looks like when she decides to write her own story.'

Stepping out into the heat, Amelia felt the sun on her new hair and smiled. Maybe it was time for all of them to remember how to live a little, to find joy in something besides duty and tradition. And if they couldn't figure it out, well . . . Japan was looking better every day.

Or perhaps, she thought, touching one vivid streak, the real adventure would be staying and being brave enough to change things from within. After all, Grandmère always said the strongest trees bend with the wind but keep their roots deep in home soil.

That thought stayed with her as she walked down the street, aware of the stares and whispers, but for once, not minding them at all.

Chapter 6

Sydney

The Sydney apartment sat fifteen storeys above a world that felt both familiar and foreign. Emily's balcony overlooked a city that never stopped moving, a stark contrast to the quiet rhythms of Duckinwilla Creek. The lights of the city contrasted with the fading light of the evening; the summer air was heavy with the scent of jasmine from her balcony pots. She sat cross-legged on her bed; Julien's letter balanced on her knee. Way below, the city thrummed with life—car horns, the wet swoosh of tyres on rain-slicked streets, the constant noise of city living. It was so different from the cicada-song evenings near the General Store, where silence was soothing, and the stars looked close enough to touch.

Her fingers traced the edge of the envelope for the hundredth time, following the familiar loops of Julien's handwriting. She'd read the letter twice already, each word a careful mix of apology and plea, but never entirely stepping into truth. The paper was starting to show wear at the creases, just like her resolve was beginning to fray at the edges.

'Damn you, Julien Johnson,' she whispered, surprised by the crack in her voice. The photo on her nightstand caught her eye—her and Julien at her cousin's wedding, his smile so open then, so unguarded. His arm was draped casually around her shoulders, that easy smile she'd fallen for lighting up his face. They'd been so happy then before the complications of Duckinwilla Creek had slowly choked the trust from their relationship.

Her phone lit up. Another message from him. Her heart jumped—traitor—even as her mind steeled itself against whatever new variation of almost-truth he'd crafted. She swiped it away, but her hand shook. That was the worst part—how her body still responded to him, how her heart still lurched at his name, how some silly part of her wanted to pretend everything was fine.

More apologies, more promises, more carefully constructed sentences that danced around the truth about Rowena. Emily's thumb hovered over the notification before she swiped it away. Even seeing his name on the screen made her heart race, and that scared her more than anything.

The balcony beckoned. Emily stepped out into the jasmine-scented night, gripping the railing as Sydney sparkled below. She missed the Creek's quiet evenings, the way sunset painted the cane fields gold, and how life moved to a gentler rhythm there. But most of all, she missed the Julien she'd first met. Now she wasn't sure where home was anymore. Part of her still longed for the quiet evenings above the General Store, just the two of them, lost in their own world.

But another part of her, the part that had built a successful teaching career and a life in Sydney, knew she couldn't go back. Not without honesty. Not without trust.

'You're stronger than this,' she told herself firmly, gripping the balcony railing.

The memory of their first meeting flooded back—that breezy autumn evening at her friend

Sarah's party when Julien's laugh had cut through the crowd with a joy of life she couldn't ignore. He'd been so genuine then, so unguarded. Their first date by the river had been a comedy of errors, with him forgetting the corkscrew for the wine and attempting to open the bottle with his car keys. They'd ended up sharing a warm beer and watching the sunset, and it had been perfect because it was real.

That's what was missing now—reality.

Her phone rang, startling her from her thoughts. It was Margot, Julien's Grandmère. Emily's stomach clenched.

'Emily, darling,' Margot's warm voice carried across the line. 'I hope I'm not disturbing you.'

'No, not at all,' Emily replied, though her grip tightened on the phone. The lie came quickly. When had she started doing that, too? She knew what was coming.

'I've been thinking about Julien,' Margot began carefully. 'He's not handling this well, *ma cherie*. Maybe if you just talked to him—'

Emily closed her eyes, fighting the urge to give

in. 'I can't, Margot. Not yet. Not until he's ready to be honest with me.'

'But surely, what happened before you were properly together—'

'It's not about what happened,' Emily cut in, surprising herself with her firmness. 'It's about the lies. Every time he denies it, every time he looks me in the eye and swears nothing happened with Rowena—that's what I can't handle. I'd forgive him in a heartbeat if he'd just tell me the truth.'

Silence stretched between them before Margot spoke again. 'Maybe you're just too different. City girl and country boy...'

The words stung, but Emily recognised the attempt to shift blame. Of course, a grandmother would be loyal to her own. 'This isn't about geography, Margot. It's about honesty. And that matters everywhere.'

After ending the call, Emily returned to her desk and pulled out a fresh sheet of paper. Her hand was steady now.

Julien, I've read your letter, and I understand

you're sorry for hurting me. But sorry isn't enough this time. I need honesty from you. Not because I want to punish you, but because without truth, there can't be trust. And without trust, there can't be us.

I've forgiven what happened with Rowena. We weren't committed then, and mistakes happen. What I can't forgive is the lying. Every denial, every avoided truth, every carefully constructed story; they're all just more walls between us.

I'm scared, Julien. I'm scared because part of me wants to pretend everything's fine, to come back to the Creek and fall back into our life together. But I'd be betraying myself if I did that. I deserve better than half-truths and careful omissions. We both do.

Until you're ready to be honest – really honest – I need to step back. Not because I don't love you, but because I do. And sometimes loving someone means being strong enough to wait for them to find their way to the truth.

Emily

She sealed the letter quickly before she could change her mind. Tomorrow, she would post it, and then . . . then she would focus on being strong enough to stand by her decision. The hardest part wasn't writing the letter or even sending it; it was knowing that Julien might show up at her door with those eyes that made her want to believe every word he said. She doubted she would have the strength to stand firm.

Emily returned to the balcony, letting the night air cool her flushed cheeks. Below, the city pulsed with life. She thought of Duckinwilla Creek, of the way the stars seemed to hang lower there, of the quiet nights and simple pleasures. She missed it all: the store, the community, the sense of belonging she'd found there. But most of all, she missed the Julien she'd first fallen in love with, the one who hadn't yet learned to hide behind careful words and half-truths.

'Come back to me,' she whispered to the night. 'Not just physically. Come back to being the man who didn't need to lie.'

Until then, she would stay here in her Sydney apartment, with its city views and familiar sounds, rebuilding her life day by day. Because love without trust was like a house built on sand. Emily had worked too hard to let everything she believed in wash away. It was time to look for some casual work at a school; her time in the north was over.

The city lights blurred as tears filled her eyes, but she didn't wipe them away. Sometimes, crying wasn't a sign of weakness—sometimes, it was proof that you were strong enough to feel everything and still stand your ground.

Chapter 7

Late afternoon sun caught the blue and orange streaks in Amelia's newly dyed hair. Charlotte had asked her to drop in to the store on the way home and help out for a couple of hours, and Amelia was happy not to go home. She was restocking the confectionery shelves when Lisette's sharp intake of breath made her turn around.

'Good Lord, what have you done to your head?' Lisette stood in the doorway; her designer sunglasses pushed up into her perfectly styled blonde hair. 'You look like a tropical parrot that had a fight with a paint tin.'

Amelia straightened, squaring her shoulders. 'It's called expressing myself, Lisette. Not that you'd understand anything that doesn't come with a designer label.'

'Expressing yourself?' Lisette's laugh was brittle. 'Bub, you look ridiculous.'

'Don't call me that!' Amelia snapped, slamming

a box of chocolate bars onto the shelf. 'I'm not twelve anymore, and you don't get to treat me like I am.'

'Well, you're certainly acting like it. What's next? A tattoo? A belly ring?'

'Maybe! And you know what else?' Amelia turned to face her sister fully. 'I'm thinking of leaving. Getting out of this gossip-soaked town and away from our crazy family.'

Lisette's perfectly shaped eyebrows rose. 'Oh, *la la*? And where exactly are you planning to go, *Bub*?'

'Japan!' The word burst out of Amelia like she'd been holding it in forever. 'I can work in a school there. Live somewhere nobody knows the Johnsons or cares about their drama.'

'Japan?' Lisette's voice dripped with derision. 'You don't even speak Japanese!'

'I can learn! Anything's better than staying here, watching everyone fall apart. Julien's lying to everyone. You and Charlotte are still at each other's throats over the store accounts, and I'm sick of it!'

Their argument was interrupted by the jangle of the bell over the door. Rowena stepped inside, hesitating when she saw the two sisters. She looked smaller somehow, less sure of herself than usual.

Lisette's attention snapped to Rowena. 'Well, well. Speaking of family drama.'

Amelia moved to leave, but Lisette grabbed her arm. 'Oh no, stay, *Bub*. You want to run away to Japan? First, let's hear what Rowena has to say about why our family's in such a mess.'

'Lisette, don't—' Rowena started, but Lisette cut her off.

'No more games, Rowena. Tell us why you've been targeting Julien. Is it the Johnson money? The family name?'

Rowena's face crumpled. 'You don't understand. None of you do! You've never had to worry about paying bills or wondering if you'll ever get out of this town!'

'So, you thought you'd use my brother as your ticket out?' Lisette's voice was razor-sharp. 'Force him into a wedding with your lies?'

'No! I love Mason!' Rowena burst out, tears springing to her eyes. 'He's everything to me. But he's a cane worker, and I'm scared. Scared of struggling forever, of never having more than what we've got right now.'

'Who's Mason?' Amelia had watched the scene unfold, her anger fading as she recognised something in Rowena's desperation—the same need to escape that had driven her to Lucy's salon.

'My boyfriend.'

'So, what's the story with Julien?'

Rowena looked cornered. 'It doesn't matter now.'

'It does, you know. You can't build a future on lies,' Amelia said quietly. 'Trust me, I've watched Julien try.'

Rowena sank onto a nearby chair, her defences crumbling. 'I know. I thought . . . I thought if Julien chose me, all my problems would be solved. I could have forgotten Mason. The Johnsons have everything: money, respect, security. But I've made such a mess of everything.'

'You're not the only one,' Lisette said, her voice softening slightly. 'This whole situation . . . it's hurt everyone. Emily, Mason, Julien. None of them deserved this.'

'I never meant for it to go this far,' Rowena whispered. 'It wasn't a total lie. Julien—'

'We don't need the details,' Lisette said sharply.

Rowena shook her head. 'I just wanted a chance at a better life. But now I might lose Mason forever.'

Amelia touched her newly coloured hair, thinking about choices and consequences. 'Sometimes we hurt the people we love most when we're trying to protect ourselves.'

Lisette shot her a look, something shifting in her expression. 'Is that why you want to run away to Japan? To protect yourself?'

'I want to *find* myself,' Amelia corrected her. 'Away from all this drama and expectations. I love our family, but sometimes love isn't enough.'

Rowena wiped her eyes. 'That's what I thought too. But running away doesn't solve anything. Whether it's being pregnant, dressing in designer clothes, or flying off to Japan—we're all just trying to escape our fears.'

The three women fell silent. The store was empty. Outside, the resident flock of galahs swooped past, their raucous calls breaking the tension.

'So, what are you going to do?' Lisette finally asked Rowena.

'Tell the truth. All of it. Mason deserves that much.' Rowena stood, squaring her shoulders. 'I need to stop trying to be something I'm not.'

Amelia felt something settle in her chest; not peace exactly, but understanding. 'Maybe we all do.'

Lisette reached out, touching one of the blue streaks in Amelia's hair. 'You know, it's actually starting to grow on me. Very . . . you.'

'Don't get soft on me now,' Amelia said, but she was smiling. 'I'm still thinking about Japan.'

'I know you are, Bub—sorry, Amelia. But maybe make sure you're running towards something, not away from it.'

'You're getting wise in your old age,' Amelia teased.

'Old, I'm not even twenty-one yet!'

The shop bell jangled again as Rowena left, seeming a little more settled.

'Why do you think she came into the store?' Lisette wondered aloud.

'To buy something, I guess. Didn't you see her face when she saw both of us?'

'I did.' Lisette stretched onto her toes.

'You were hard on her, but at least it made her think about her choices.'

'Want to get Friday night fish and chips for dinner and sit by the creek?' Lisette asked suddenly. 'We can talk about this Japan thing properly. No judgement, I promise.'

Amelia hesitated, then nodded. 'Okay. But if you call me Bub one more time, I'm dyeing your hair while you sleep.'

They waited until Charlotte came back in from the storeroom. Her eyes widened as she saw them chatting civilly.

'We're off to Mac's Fish and Chips for tea. Do you want anything?' Amelia asked.

Charlotte shook her head. 'No, thanks. Greg's cooking tonight.' Her smile was dreamy; she'd been off with the fairies most of the day.

'Where is Greg? Isn't it time to shut up shop?'

'He went to Dunmora to visit his parents this afternoon, and then he was going straight back to *Maison de Rêve*.'

Amelia giggled as they stepped out into the cooling evening air.

'What?'

'Look at the colour of the sky. Same orange as my hair.'

The sun was setting behind the cane fields, painting the sky in shades that almost matched Amelia's hair.

'I can't wait to see Mum's reaction,' Lisette said smugly.

'Don't start. I don't have to eat tea with you,' Amelia snapped.

'Well, you know she's going to go off.'

'I'm eighteen. I can do what I like now.'

'Did you see Charlotte and Greg before he left this morning?' Amelia asked as they walked towards the takeaway store. 'They were practically dancing around each other in the stockroom.'

Lisette's nose wrinkled slightly. 'Oh yes, the great romance of Duckinwilla Creek. It's like watching a Mills and Boon novel come to life.'

'You're just jealous,' Amelia said, grinning at her sister's obvious discomfort.

'Jealous? Of what? The way they finish each other's sentences? The sickeningly sweet looks? The constant hand-holding?'

'The fact that they're happy,' Amelia said softly. 'That they found each other without any drama or complications. I do hope they get engaged soon.'

Lisette was quiet for a moment, her heels clicking on the pavement. 'I did see Greg helping Charlotte with the monthly accounts yesterday. He brought her coffee and sat there for two hours, just . . being there. Who does that?'

'Someone in love,' Amelia replied.

'At least some things in this family worked out right,' Lisette said, pushing open the door of Mac's café.

They joined the queue at the counter. Lisette studied the menu on the board above them with unnecessary intensity.

'You know,' she said finally, staring at the board. 'I always thought I'd be the first one to find that. The whole happy-ever-after thing.'

'You're always out with someone, though.'

'Yes, but they don't want me,' Lisette protested. 'They're chasing the idea of me. The Johnson name, the family business. No one brings me coffee and just sits with me.'

Amelia reached across the table, squeezing her sister's hand. 'Maybe because you don't let them.'

'Maybe,' Lisette admitted. 'But it's easier this way. Safer. Look at what happened with Julien and Emily.'

'Is that why you're so hard on everyone? Because you're scared of getting hurt?'

Lisette's perfectly made-up face softened. 'Is that why you want to run away to Japan? Because you're scared of staying?'

'Touché,' Amelia laughed. 'Look at us, the Johnson sisters. One hiding behind her designer clothes and make-up, one hiding behind crazy hair dye, and Charlotte—'

'Charlotte just being Charlotte in love,' Lisette finished. 'Growing up away from us.'

They ordered their takeaway and found a table near the creek where a soft breeze ruffled the water, their conversation flowing easier than it ever had.

'You know,' Lisette said, holding up a chip, 'if you really want to go to Japan, I could help you. Look for some language courses, find out what qualifications you need and how you can get them, whatever you need.'

Amelia looked at her sister in surprise. 'Really? No lecture about family duty?'

'Maybe watching Charlotte and Greg has taught me something. Sometimes, you have to let people find their own way.' Lisette smirked. 'Even if that way involves ridiculous hair.'

'Don't start,' Amelia warned, but she was smiling. 'Tomorrow, we have to deal with this Rowena situation.'

'And Julien, and help Charlotte at the store and make sure Dad really is okay.' Lisette sighed. 'But tonight, maybe we can just be sisters.'

'Sisters with great hair,' Amelia corrected, making Lisette laugh.

'One sister with great hair, one with a tropical disaster on her head,' Lisette teased. 'But yes, just sisters.'

They burst out laughing. Their laughter was unexpected—a shared recognition of the absurdity of their Johnson family dynamics. Lisette's usual snort startled an old man reading at the next table; he looked up and then quickly back down, pretending he hadn't noticed.

As they sat at the table by the creek, the warm evening wrapped around them like a cocoon. Outside, Duckinwilla Creek settled into its nightly routine, but for once, neither sister was in a hurry to rejoin it.

Chapter 8

Lisette woke to the sound of Amelia singing in the shower—some pop song massacred with deliberate cheerfulness. She rolled over, burying her face in her pillow to hide her smile. The memory of last night still felt fragile, like a soap bubble that might burst if she examined it too closely: sitting by the creek with her little sister, really talking for the first time in years.

Her phone buzzed—another message from Charlotte about the store's accounts. Lisette started to type her usual sharp response, then stopped and deleted it. She thought about what Amelia had said about hiding behind designer clothes and cutting remarks. Maybe it was time to try something different.

Coming in early to help with those numbers.

She hit send before she could second-guess herself. The bathroom door opened in a cloud of steam, and Amelia emerged, her blue and orange hair wrapped in one of Mum's best white towels. 'You're going to give Mum a heart attack with that towel,' Lisette said, but without her usual bite. 'The dye will stain it.'

'Already checked. It's colourfast now.' Amelia flopped onto Lisette's bed, damp and warm. 'What are you doing today?'

'Store accounts with Charlotte.' Lisette watched her sister's eyebrows rise. 'What? I can be helpful.'

'I know you can. You just usually choose not to be.'

The words should have stung, but they didn't. Maybe because Amelia said them without judgment, just stating a fact like commenting on the weather or noting the time.

'Well, people can change.' Lisette sat up, reaching for her hairbrush. 'Speaking of which, I did some online research. There's a language school in Brisbane that offers intensive Japanese courses. Three months, live-in accommodation included.'

Amelia went still. 'You're serious about helping me?'

'Of course, I am.' Lisette focused on brushing her hair, not meeting her sister's eyes. 'But you have to be serious too. No more spur-of-the-moment fixes like—' she waved her brush at Amelia's hair '—this.'

'Hey, I love my hair!'

'And I love that you love it,' Lisette surprised herself by saying. 'But Japan isn't a hair appointment. It's your life.'

Amelia was quiet for a moment, picking at Lisette's duvet cover. 'You know what scares me most? That I'll get there and fail. That everyone will say, "I told you so," and I'll have to come crawling back.'

Lisette set down her brush. 'Then don't fail.'

'That simple, huh?'

'No.' Lisette turned to face her sister properly. 'But you've got something now you didn't have before.'

'What's that?'

'Me.' She shrugged at Amelia's startled look. 'And Charlotte. And even Greg, probably, since he's practically family now. We've got your back.'

Amelia's eyes filled with tears. 'When did you get so nice?'

'Don't spread it around. I have a reputation to maintain.' Lisette stood, moving to her closet. 'Now, help me pick something to wear suitable for accounting.'

'Everything you own is suitable for everything,' Amelia groaned, but she got up to look. 'You're like a walking designer catalogue.'

'Yes, well—' Lisette fingered the silk of her favourite blouse. 'Maybe it's time I learned to be comfortable in something less perfect.'

'Lisette Johnson, was that personal growth I just witnessed?'

'Shut up and help me choose.'

They settled on a simple sundress—still designer but softer than Lisette's usual armour-like blazers and pencil skirts. As they headed downstairs, Amelia surprised her by linking their arms.

'You know,' Amelia said as they walked into the kitchen. 'I might wait on Japan—just until things settle here. I want to see how this new sister thing works out.'

'Good.' Lisette squeezed her arm. 'Because I'd miss you, you tropical disaster.'

'I'd miss you too, you designer snob.'

Oliver was already at the kitchen table, hunched over his breakfast and scrolling through what was probably a weather app on his phone. He looked up as they entered, though his eyebrows lifted slightly at their linked arms.

Their mother set down her coffee, eyes widening at their easy smiles. 'Well,' she said carefully, 'this is new.'

'Not new,' Lisette corrected, reaching for the coffee pot. Then, unable to resist, she peered over Oliver's shoulder. 'Please tell me you're looking at something more exciting than rainfall predictions.'

'Mango market prices, actually,' Oliver muttered, tilting the phone away from her. 'Some of us have real work to do.'

'Oh yes, because managing the store isn't real work.' Lisette ruffled his hair as she passed, knowing it would annoy him. 'When was the last time you went on a date, dear brother? Or are you married to those cane fields?'

'Leave him alone,' Amelia said, but she was grinning. 'Not everyone needs to be seen at every social event in a hundred-kilometre radius.'

Oliver shot her a grateful look, then did a double-take at her hair. 'Speaking of being seen, did your head fight with a paint factory?'

'You're about twelve hours too late with that line,' Amelia said, stealing a piece of his toast. 'Lisette already covered the tropical parrot references.'

'At least I got out of bed after dawn to make jokes,' Lisette said, sliding into her chair. 'Unlike some farmers I could mention.'

'I've only been up since four,' Oliver protested. 'Some of us actually work for a living instead of just ordering people around in designer heels.'

'Children,' their mother warned, but there was a slight hint of a smile on her face. A slight hint. It had been a while since their bickering had this much fun to it.

'You know,' Lisette said thoughtfully, stirring her coffee, 'if you let me set you up with Sarah from the bank—'

'No,' Oliver cut her off. 'Absolutely not. The last time you played matchmaker I ended up stuck at dinner with someone who thought cane was just something you put in wicker furniture.'

'Your standards are impossible,' Lisette sighed dramatically. 'So, she just needs to know the difference between sugar cane and bamboo?'

'And understand agricultural futures, irrigation systems, and sustainable farming practices,' Oliver added seriously.

'Good lord, it's a date, not a job interview,' Lisette groaned.

Later, parking at the back of the store, Lisette thought about changes—how they could happen in an instant, like Amelia's hair, or slowly, like the growing peace between sisters. She thought about Charlotte waiting at the store with her quiet determination. About Greg's patient presence and

Julien's messy absence. About Rowena's desperate grab for security and her own carefully constructed walls.

Her phone buzzed with a text from Amelia: **Found some online Japanese lessons. Want to help me practise tonight?**

Lisette smiled, typing back: **Only if you help me learn to be less perfect.**

Deal, came the reply. **But I'm not dyeing your hair.**

Thank God for small mercies, Lisette sent back and then added, **Love you, tropical disaster.**

The response was immediate: **Love you too, designer snob.**

Pulling up outside the store, Lisette caught sight of her reflection in the rear-view mirror. It showed the same perfectly styled hair and the same flawless makeup. But something was different. Something in her eyes, maybe. Or something in her heart.

Change, she was learning, didn't always need to be as dramatic as blue and orange hair. Sometimes, it was as simple as letting down a wall, brick by careful brick, until you could finally see what was on the other side.

Chapter 9

The morning rush at *Bean There Coffee* was in full swing, and Emily's fingers ached from tamping coffee grounds. A month ago, she'd been helping run a successful family business in Duckinwilla Creek. Now, she was making five different complicated coffee orders for suited-up bankers who couldn't even be bothered to look up from their phones when they ordered. She'd barely had a spare moment to look at the casual vacancies; the sooner she could get back into teaching the better. She'd kidded herself that working in a coffee shop would be like working with Julien at the General Store.

Boy, had she been wrong.

'Large soy cappuccino, extra hot, no foam!' The order barker, Kelly, called out. 'And hurry up with that bank order; they called twice already!'

Emily bit back a retort. At the General Store, she'd managed inventory, handled accounts, and made decisions that actually mattered. Here, she couldn't even suggest a more efficient way to handle multiple orders without Kelly reminding her she was "just a barista".

The bell above the door chimed, and Emily's heart stopped. She didn't need to look up to know who had just walked in—after months together, she'd sense Julien's presence anywhere. She ducked behind the massive espresso machine, grateful for its bulky presence.

Through the steam and chrome, she caught glimpses of him. He looked terrible: unshaven, with dark circles under his eyes, and his usually neat clothes were crumpled. The sight of him made her chest ache, but she pushed the feeling away, focusing on the banking order. Large flat white, two sugars. Skim latte, extra hot. Macchiato, no sugar—

'Hey there, coffee girl.'

Emily looked up to find herself face to face with a tall guy in board shorts and a tank top, salt-crusted hair falling over one eye. He leaned against the counter, peering over the machine and flashing what he clearly thought was a winning smile.

'Can I help you?' Emily asked, keeping her tone

professional.

'Definitely. How about your number for starters?' He grinned wider. 'I'm Micko. I've seen you here before. I always wanted to say hi.'

'No, you haven't. I've just started here, and I'm working,' Emily said firmly, turning back to the coffee machine. Fifth order: long black, no sugar.

'Come on, don't be like that. One coffee, that's all I'm asking. When do you get off?'

'She said she's working.'

Emily closed her eyes briefly at the sound of Julien's voice, low and firm. When she opened them, he was standing at the counter, and the difference between him and Micko was stark. Even rumpled and tired, Julien carried himself with the quiet confidence she'd first fallen for.

'Mate, I'm just being friendly,' Micko protested.

'No, you're harassing someone who's trying to do her job.' Julien's voice was quiet but carried an edge Emily recognised from dealing with difficult customers at the store.

Micko looked between them, understanding dawning. 'Oh, right. Should've known a pretty thing like you'd be taken. Whatever.' He pushed off from the counter. 'Your loss, coffee girl!'

The silence that followed felt thick enough to cut. Emily focused on finishing the banking order, very aware of Julien's presence.

'Long black, please,' he said finally. 'And . . . Emily? Can we talk? I'm heading back to the Creek today, but I'd like to say goodbye properly.'

Emily's hands shook slightly as she worked the machine. 'Don't think you can soften me up just because you played white knight with surfer boy.'

'That's not what I'm trying to do.'

She risked a glance at him and immediately wished she hadn't. His eyes held the same warmth they always had, and for a moment, she was back in Duckinwilla Creek, planning their future together. She looked away quickly.

'Your coffee will be ready in a minute,' she said, her voice clipped. 'Have a safe trip home.'

'Em, please—'

'Kelly,' Emily called out, already backing toward the staff door. 'I need to check supplies. Can you handle the orders, please?'

She didn't wait for an answer, pushing through the door into the back room. She stood there in the semi-darkness, surrounded by boxes of coffee beans and paper cups, trying to steady her breathing. Through the door, she heard Kelly's voice. 'Sorry, she's busy with inventory.' She was a good friend.

Emily pressed her hands against her eyes, fighting back tears. She thought she was stronger than this, thought she could handle seeing Julien. But one look, one moment of connection, and all her carefully built walls threatened to crumble.

'Get it together,' she whispered to herself. 'He hasn't changed. He's still lying.'

But as she heard the bell chime again, signalling Julien's departure, she couldn't help but remember the way he'd looked at her, like she was still the most important person in his world. She stayed in the storeroom until she was sure he'd left, then squared her shoulders and went back out to face another day of coffee orders and condescending customers.

At least making coffee was simpler than untangling her heart.

***

Julien stood outside *Bean There Coffee* for ten more minutes, his untouched coffee growing cold in his hands. The surge of anger he'd felt when that surfer guy started hitting on Emily had shocked him. He'd wanted to do more than just warn the guy off— he'd wanted to grab him by his faded singlet top and throw him out the door. The violence of that impulse scared him.

He dropped the full cup in a nearby bin and ran his hands through his unwashed hair. When had he become this person? Three days of stubble on his chin, rum on his breath from last night, and clothes that looked like he'd slept in them— because he had. His car was littered with takeaway containers and empty beer bottles.

'Come on, Em,' he muttered, watching the door. 'Just give me five minutes.'

Through the window, he could see her friend

Kelly efficiently working the coffee machine. No sign of Emily. He knew he was being a stalker; he knew he should just get in his ute and start the long drive home. But the thought of leaving Sydney without trying again made his chest tight.

A customer came out, the bell tinkling. For a moment, he caught the scent of coffee and vanilla—the same scent that used to fill their flat above the store when Emily baked. The memory hit him like a punch to the gut.

Just tell her the truth.

The thought surfaced like it had a hundred times before, but he pushed it away. If he admitted to sleeping with Rowena, Emily would never forgive him. Better to keep denying it, go home, give her time to miss him. She loved him—he'd seen it in her eyes just now before she looked away. That had to be enough.

Didn't it?

After twenty minutes, it became clear Emily wasn't coming out. Julien walked the three blocks to where he'd parked his ute, each step feeling heavier than the last. The familiar blue Hilux looked out of place among the sleek city cars. Like him—a country boy pretending he belonged in Sydney. How had he ever thought he wanted to live here and be a chef? He must have had rocks in his head.

He climbed in, the leather seat creaking under him. The dashboard was dusty from his drive down, and Emily's water bottle was still on the floor. He should clean the rubbish up, but somehow, he couldn't bring himself to erase that last trace of her.

The engine rumbled to life, and Julien pulled into the morning traffic. As the city buildings rose around him like a glass and steel prison, he thought about the long drive ahead. Two days on the road, just him and his thoughts. Maybe by the time he got home, he'd have figured out how to fix this mess.

You know how to fix it, a voice in his head that sounded suspiciously like Charlotte whispered. *Stop lying.*

'Shut up,' he muttered, turning onto the motorway that would take him north. The morning sun hit his windscreen, nearly blinding him. He fumbled for his sunglasses, finding them under a receipt from the bottle shop.

God, he was a mess. The rage he'd felt at the surfer, the drinking, the lying; it was all spiralling out of control. But the thought of losing Emily forever terrified him more than his own self-destruction.

The city thinned out around him as he headed north. Soon, the skyscrapers would give way to suburbs and then to the endless stretches of highway that would lead him home to Duckinwilla Creek. To the store, to his family, to all the complications he'd been trying to escape in Sydney.

But not to Emily.

He pressed harder on the accelerator as if he could outrun the truth trying to catch up with him. The ute's engine growled in response, eating up the kilometres. His phone buzzed; Charlotte was probably checking on him again. He ignored it.

Two days. Two days of driving through the countryside that would remind him of Emily with every turn. The roadside cafés where they'd stopped on their drive to Duckinwilla Creek that first road trip. The lookout where they'd watched the sunrise. The small towns where she'd insisted on trying every local bakery.

'She'll come back,' he told himself, merging onto the Pacific Motorway. 'Once she realises how much she misses the Creek. Misses me.'

But as Sydney disappeared in his rear-view mirror, another thought surfaced, unwanted but persistent: What if she didn't? What if his lies had finally cost him the one person he couldn't bear to lose?

Julien cranked up the radio, trying to drown out his thoughts with country music. But every love song, every heartbreak ballad, just reminded him of what he was running from. And what he was running to.

His phone buzzed through the car speakers. Charlotte's name lit up the display. Julien hit the Bluetooth button on his steering wheel, grateful for the interruption to his depressing thoughts.

'Hey, Charlie.'

'Jules? Where are you? Are you okay?'

'On the way back.' He squinted at a road sign as it flashed past. 'Just passed Wyong. And no, not really.'

'What's wrong? What's happened?'

'Nothing. I just thought—' He watched a flock of black cockatoos sweep across the highway. 'I thought if I denied it long enough, it would go away. That Emily would believe me eventually.'

'How's that working out?' Charlotte's tone was pointed but not unkind.

'About as well as you'd expect.' He managed a hollow laugh. 'I'm driving back to the Creek alone, aren't I?'

'There's a letter here for you. Looks like Emily's writing.'

'I could have saved myself a trip,' he said bitterly.

'Come home,' Charlotte said softly. 'We'll figure it out together. But Julien? No more lies. Promise me.'

He hesitated, watching the highway stretch

ahead of him like a future without Emily. 'I'll try, Charlie.'

After they hung up, the highway stretched ahead of him, a ribbon of bitumen leading back to Duckinwilla Creek. Back to the mess he'd made. Back to a home that wouldn't feel like home without Emily in it.

He had two days of driving to figure out his next move. Two days to decide if he was brave enough to tell the truth or if he'd keep building his house of lies until it finally collapsed around him.

The sun climbed higher as he drove north, and somewhere behind him, in a Sydney coffee shop, Emily was probably already forgetting about their brief encounter. Probably laughing with customers, moving on with her life.

Julien pressed the accelerator a little harder as if the extra speed could somehow keep his world from falling apart.

Chapter 10

'You can't hide up here forever.' Charlotte's voice drifted up the narrow staircase to the flat above the store.

Julien stared at the ceiling, counting water stains. 'Not hiding.'

'Really?' The stairs creaked beneath her feet. 'Because that's exactly what it looks like to everyone in town.'

'Since when do you care what everyone thinks?'

Charlotte appeared in the doorway, hands on hips. The gesture was so similar to their mother's that Julien had to look away. Empty bourbon bottles lined the windowsill where Emily's herb garden used to be. The sight made his stomach turn.

'Since Lucy Lou cornered me at the post office to ask if you were "having some sort of breakdown."' Charlotte crossed to the window, yanking open the curtains. 'Since Dad's blood pressure went up again with the stress. Since you decided that sleeping off hangovers was better than facing your problems. Not a good look.'

Julien pushed himself up off the sofa, self-disgust flooding him. He finally looked up, catching his reflection in the window. A stranger stared back—unshaven, defeated, a ghost of the man he'd once been.

When did he turn into such a weak specimen?

Sunlight flooded the small room, highlighting empty takeaway containers from Mac's and unwashed clothes. He squinted against the brightness, his head pounding. He couldn't remember when he'd last eaten anything that hadn't come in a plastic container or a paper bag.

'I didn't decide anything,' he said quietly. 'It just . . . happened.'

'Bullshit.' Charlotte's voice cracked. '*You* chose to lie to Emily. *You* chose to mess around with Rowena. *You* chose to throw away everything good in your life because you were too scared to admit you were happy here.'

Down below, he could hear Greg working in the store—the familiar rhythm of the bell jangling over the door, the murmur of conversation with customers. His store, once. His life, once. Now, the counter where Emily had worked by his side was being managed by someone else.

'Grandmère wants everyone at their place tonight,' Charlotte said after a moment. 'And I mean *everyone*.'

Julien's stomach clenched. 'Everyone?'

'The whole family.' Charlotte picked up a dirty mug, grimacing at the mould inside. 'Grandmère's making her *coq au vin*.'

'I can't.'

'You can.' Charlotte's tone left no room for argument. 'And you're going to the preschool to tell Amelia for me. I'm too busy to run down there while you're wallowing in your misery up here. It's time to man up, Julien.'

He shot up from the couch. 'What? No. Just text her.'

'Everyone else got the summons in person. You need to get out of this flat, and Amelia needs to hear it from family.' Charlotte's eyes softened slightly.

'Besides, those kids from the preschool miss their lolly man.'

The thought of walking through town, facing the whispers and stares, made his chest tight. But Charlotte was right—he couldn't hide forever.

'Fine,' he muttered. 'I'll go.'

'Shower first. You smell like the pub floor.'

The walk to the preschool was like running a gauntlet. Mrs Thompson clutched her handbag closer when he passed. Old Mr Peters suddenly found his shoelaces fascinating. Through the newsagent's window, he could see Lucy Lou's head bent close to Jerry's, both of them watching him pass.

The preschool's bright murals and cheerful gate felt like another world. Through the fence, he could see Amelia in the playground, the newly dyed hair he'd heard about living up to everything that had been said. She helped a small boy down the slide and looked up at his approach, her smile faltering slightly.

'Hello, stranger.' Amelia came to the fence.

'What are you doing here?'

'Dinner at Grandmère's tonight,' he said, his voice rough. 'Grandmère's orders.'

Before Amelia could respond, a small voice piped up: 'Mr Julien! Did you bring lollies?'

He turned to find Sophie, one of his regular customers, looking up at him hopefully through the fence. Behind her, other children were starting to notice him, faces lighting up with recognition.

'Not today, sweetheart,' he managed.

'When are you coming back to the store?' another child asked. 'Mummy says the new lollies aren't as good as the lolly man's.'

Julien felt something crack in his chest. These kids, their simple acceptance, their uncomplicated joy in sugar and kindness—it was everything he'd walked away from.

'Soon,' he found himself saying. 'Maybe soon.'

Chapter 11

Julien left the preschool, the children's voices fading behind him. He walked slowly, seeing his hometown as a stranger might: the neat shopfronts with their striped awnings, the jacaranda trees dropping purple petals on the footpath, the way everyone seemed to know everyone else's business.

Rowena saw him and froze, her face flushing. 'Julien,' she said, her voice barely above a whisper. 'Can we talk? Please? Just for a minute.'

Through the salon window, Lucy watched, her rainbow-striped apron a stark contrast to her stern expression. Mabel from the newsagent had slowed her pace, probably already planning tomorrow's gossip.

'I don't think that's a good idea, Rowena.' His voice came out harsher than he'd intended. The sight of her made his stomach turn—not with desire anymore but with shame.

'I know I have no right to ask, but—' She wrapped her arms around herself. 'There are things we need to sort out. About what I said.'

He pushed past her into Lucy's salon, the bell jingling overhead. The familiar scent of hair dye and coffee hit him—how many times had he ducked in here as a kid, stealing lollies from Lucy's jar while she did his mum's hair?

'Well, if it isn't the talk of the town.' Lucy's voice carried across the empty salon. 'Come to confess your sins?'

'I'm looking for Amelia,' he lied, though they both knew he was escaping the confrontation with Rowena.

'Your sister's got better things to do than clean up your mess.' Lucy crossed her arms. 'I've known you since you were knee-high to a grasshopper, Julien Johnson. Used to do your mother's hair every Friday, and she'd tell me about her dreams for you all.'

The mention of his mother made him wince. Every Friday, without fail, she'd sit in that chair by the window, planning futures for her children that none of them had entirely lived up to.

Yet.

'Charlotte, the responsible one. Lisette, the ambitious one. Oliver, steady as a rock. And you—you were supposed to be the heart of the family.' Lucy shook her head. 'What happened to that boy, Julien? The one who used to help old Mrs. James carry her groceries even when his friends teased him about it?'

Through the window, he could see his old life playing out without him: Charlotte and Greg at the store, Mrs Thompson gossiping outside the post office, and the school bus picking up kids who would have once made a beeline for his lolly counter. The town moved on while he stood still, trapped in the mess he'd made.

'I don't know how to fix this,' he admitted.

'Maybe you can't.' Lucy's voice softened. 'Maybe some things aren't meant to be fixed. Maybe they're meant to be learned from.' She pointed her comb at him. 'Look in that mirror, Julien. Really look. Because right now, you're not just losing Emily. You're losing yourself.'

He forced himself to look—really look—at his reflection. Three days of stubble, shadows under his eyes, defeat was written in every line. Behind him in the mirror, Duckinwilla Creek went about its business, the afternoon light turning everything golden. He remembered other afternoons, standing behind the counter of his store, watching this same light paint Emily's hair copper as she laughed at his terrible jokes.

'The truth is,' Lucy said, 'you know Amelia understands Emily better. You need to talk to her because she understands *you* better. She sees the good in everyone, just like Emily does. And right now, you need someone to remind you that there's still good in you under all these lies. The truth might hurt, love, but lies will kill you slowly. Your choice which pain you want to live with.'

As Julien stepped out of the salon, Lucy's final words followed him. He walked slowly along Main Street with no destination in mind. Past the places that held his memories—good and bad. The store where he and Emily had worked side by side, the creek bank where they'd planned their future. The bench where he'd first noticed Rowena looking at him differently and made the choice that would cost him everything.

Rowena's accusation: the catalyst for him spiralling down.

Maybe Lucy was right. Perhaps some things couldn't be fixed. But maybe, just maybe, they could be rebuilt differently but stronger. Starting with dinner at Grandmère's and the truth he'd been running from for too long.

Lucy's words echoed in his mind all the way back to the flat. An hour later, showered, shaved, and wearing the only clean shirt he could find in his cupboard, he didn't hesitate at the door to Jerry's Barber Shop; he just walked straight in. Jerry looked up, surprise flickering across his weathered face, but said nothing as he gestured to the empty chair.

Julien caught Lucy's approving nod through the salon window as he left with a decent haircut half an hour later.

Chapter 12

The gravel crunched under Julien's feet as he walked up the long drive to his grandparents' new home. The French provincial house loomed against the darkening sky. Through the windows he could see people moving and hear the murmur of voices and clinking of glasses.

Grandmère was waiting on the verandah, her petite figure straight as ever in her navy dress. The look she gave him stopped him at the bottom of the stairs.

'The others are in the kitchen,' she said quietly. 'Come with me.'

She led him around the side of the house to her rose garden. The air was heavy with their scent, mixed with coming rain. They settled on the old bench beneath the climbing Pierre de Ronsard roses, their pale pink blooms nodding in the evening breeze.

'Your grandfather built this bench when we lived at *Maison de Rêve*,' Grandmère said, running her hand along the weathered wood. 'Do you know why?'

Julien shook his head.

'Because I told him I needed a place to think. A place to make the hard decisions. I brought it here with us.' She turned to face him fully. 'Do you know what the hardest decision is, *mon petit*?'

'Leaving?' His voice was barely a whisper.

'*Non.*' Her voice sharpened. 'The hardest decision is staying. Choosing to face what you've done instead of running away. Choosing to be honest when lies would be easier.' She reached for his hand, her grip surprisingly strong. 'You are not the first person to make mistakes, Julien. But you might be the first in this family to let those mistakes destroy you.'

'I've ruined everything, Grandmère.'

'Perhaps.' She was quiet for a moment. 'Or perhaps you needed to break everything to see what was truly valuable. Tell me, when you were in Sydney, what did you miss most?'

The answer came without thinking. 'Sunday

mornings at the store. The kids coming in after school. Emily's laugh when I'd try out new recipes—'

'Ah.' Grandmère's eyes were knowing. 'Not the excitement? Not the big city dreams?'

'No,' he admitted.

'Then perhaps you're not as lost as you think.' She stood, straightening her dress. 'But Julien? No more hiding in that flat. No more drinking instead of feeling. And no more lies—to yourself or anyone else. *C'est compris?*'

'*Oui*, Grandmère.'

'Good.' She cupped his cheek in her hand. 'Now, you will come inside. You will face your family. You will eat my *coq au vin*. And tomorrow, you will start cleaning up the mess you've made— both in that flat and in this town.'

Julien shook his head; how did Grandmère know everything that was going on all the time? She hadn't even been in the flat.

Thunder rumbled in the distance as they walked back to the house. Through the kitchen window,

Julien could see his family moving around: Charlotte leaning against Greg, Amelia setting the table, and his parents talking quietly in the corner. The sight made his chest ache with longing.

'They're still your family,' Grandmère said softly. 'Even when you don't deserve them.'

The first drops of rain began to fall as they climbed the stairs. Julien paused at the door, the warmth and light spilling out around him. Maybe Grandmère was right. Maybe staying was the hardest choice—but perhaps it was also the only one that mattered.

Chapter 13

Emily had been staring at her phone for the past hour, watching it light up with Julien's calls, each one sending a fresh wave of anger and disappointment through her chest. Outside, the city hummed with its usual energy, but up here on the fifteenth floor, Emily felt removed from it all, suspended in a moment of decision.

When the phone buzzed again, she finally answered it.

'Emily.' Julien's voice was firm. 'I need to tell you something. I read your letter. It's made me wake up to myself.'

She closed her eyes, pressing her forehead against the cool glass of her window. 'Let me guess. You finally remembered you slept with Rowena.'

The sharp intake of breath on the other end told her she'd caught him off guard. 'How did you—'

'I always knew.' Emily watched a sparrow hop on her balcony, chasing the toast crumbs from her breakfast. 'But that's not really the point, is it?' She turned away from the window, pacing across her polished floorboards. 'The point is you lied to me when I asked you about it.'

The silence on the other end stretched out like the dusty roads of Duckinwilla Creek.

'Emily, I—'

'I already knew the truth when we talked, Julien.' Her voice came out steadier than she felt.

Another pause, this one heavy with realisation. 'Why didn't you tell me you knew?'

Emily sank onto her couch, running her fingers through her dark hair. The setting sun caught the rose gold watch Julien had given her for her birthday, making it glint accusingly. 'Because it happened before we were serious. Before you asked me to move to Duckinwilla with you. What happened with Rowena upset me, but we weren't exclusive then.'

'You . . . forgave me?'

'Yes. There was nothing to forgive there.' Emily's throat tightened. 'But I can't forgive you for lying to me. Every time you denied it, every time you looked me in the eye and swore nothing happened—that's what I can't get past.'

'I was scared,' Julien's voice cracked. 'When the pregnancy rumour started, I panicked. I thought if you knew about that night with Rowena—'

'You thought I'd leave you?' Emily stood up again, unable to keep still. 'I loved you, Julien. I left Sydney, my job, and everything I've built here to go to Duckinwilla Creek. For you. Because I thought we had something real.'

'We do have something real.' The desperation in his voice made her heart ache. 'Emily, please. I love you. I'll do anything—'

'Love isn't enough without trust.' She moved back to the window, watching the sky turn purple over the harbour. 'You've been lying to me for months. Not just about Rowena, but about everything. Your worries, your feelings. You always pretended everything was fine, but I could see you weren't. Every time you had the chance to come clean, you chose to lie instead.'

'I didn't want to lose you.'

'And how's that working out?' The words came out sharper than she intended, but she couldn't soften them now. 'You know what hurts the most? I would have understood. God, Julien, I grew up in a small town. I know how these things happen. One night at the pub, too many drinks, old history . . . I get it. But you didn't trust me enough to tell me the truth. Or to share your inner feelings with me.'

She could picture him there, surrounded by the technicolour sunset of the creek, the cane fields stretching out beyond the General Store like a green sea.

'I've made such a mess of everything,' he said finally.

'Yes, you have.' Emily watched a ferry cut across the harbour, its lights bright against the darkening water.

'Tell me what to do. Please, Em. I'll do anything.'

'I don't know how to fix it.' She closed her eyes, remembering the way he'd looked at her the first time she visited the Creek, how he'd shown her his favourite spot by the water, the way he'd talked about their future. The memory hurt now, tainted by all the lies that had followed.

'And I can't tell you what to do, Julien. That's part of the problem. You need to figure out who you want to be—the man who keeps lying to protect himself, or someone better than that.'

'I want to be better. For you.'

'No.' Emily's voice was firm. 'Not for me. For yourself. Because until you can be honest about who you are and what you've done, nothing between us will ever work.'

The silence that followed was broken only by the distant sound of kookaburras marking the sunset in Duckinwilla Creek.

'I'm so sorry, Emily.'

'I know you are.' She touched the cool glass of her window, remembering the heat of the country, the way the air shimmered above the cane fields. 'But sorry isn't enough this time.'

'Are you saying we're over?'

Emily watched her reflection in the darkening

window, seeing the strength in her own eyes that had taken so long to find. 'I'm saying I need time. And you need to decide who you really are, Julien Johnson. Because the man I fell in love with wouldn't have kept lying to me, even when the truth got hard.'

She heard him draw in a shaky breath. 'I love you, Em.'

'I love you too.' Her voice softened. 'That's what makes this so hard. But I won't build a life on lies, Julien. Not even for you.'

After she hung up, Emily stood at her window for a long time, watching the city lights come alive below her. Somewhere in the distance, a horn echoed mournfully in the harbour, reminding her of the whistle of wind through the cane fields. She thought about Julien, sitting outside the store in Duckinwilla Creek, watching the same stars beginning to appear in the darkening sky.

Love wasn't the problem. It never had been. But trust, once broken, was like the creek itself after a storm—it needed time to settle, to run clear again.

Whether their love was strong enough to wait for that clearing, only time would tell.

Chapter 14

The late afternoon sun slanted through the windows of Rowena's flat, the harsh Queensland light making Julien feel exposed, vulnerable. He hadn't wanted to come here; Rowena meant facing all his mistakes, all his lies. But Charlotte had been insistent, and when his sister got that tone in her voice, resistance was futile.

'Sit down, Julien,' Charlotte commanded, and he found himself obeying automatically, sinking into the worn armchair. Rowena perched on the edge of her couch, Charlotte and Lisette flanking her like sentries.

'We need to sort this out,' Lisette said, her usual sharp edges softened by concern. 'All of it. No more hiding.'

Julien's chest felt tight. Emily's words from their last conversation echoed in his head: "I love you, but I can't trust you." The memory made him want to curl in on himself.

'I've already lost her,' he said, his voice hollow. 'What's the point?'

'The point,' Lisette snapped, 'is that you're not the only one who's been hiding from the truth. Is he, Rowena?'

Rowena twisted her hands in her lap. 'No,' she whispered.

The sound of heavy footsteps in the hallway made them all look up. Mason appeared in the doorway, his presence making the flat feel even more confined. His face darkened when he saw Julien.

'What's this?' he demanded. 'Some kind of reconciliation?'

'Mason, wait—' Rowena stood, but he was already turning away.

'No need to explain. Guess the rumours were true after all.'

'They weren't,' Julien said quickly, suddenly desperate to clear at least this truth. 'None of them. That's why I'm here.'

Rowena burst into tears. 'Just listen to me,

okay?'

What followed was a painful excavation of truth: the drunken night that meant nothing, the rumours Rowena had let spread, the lie Julien had told to protect himself. He closed his eyes as she kept talking, and his guilt grew.

'I let you believe the baby might be yours, Julien,' Rowena admitted, tears streaming. 'Because I was scared of struggling, of never having security. I saw what the Johnsons had, and I . . . I was weak.'

'While I was working to build our future,' Mason said bitterly as he headed to the door. 'Taking management courses, planning our life together.'

The words hit Julien like physical blows. He'd been so caught up in protecting his relationship with Emily that he'd never stopped to think about anyone else.

'Julien? Your turn.' Charlotte's voice was gentle but firm. 'Why didn't you tell Emily the truth from the start?'

Julien ran a hand through his hair, feeling the familiar shame rise. 'Because I was terrified,' he admitted. 'Every time I thought about telling her, I imagined her walking away. So, I kept lying, thinking if I denied it enough, it would just . . . go away.' He laughed bitterly. 'And now she's gone anyway.'

'You're going to give up that easily?' Lisette challenged. 'The brother I grew up with wouldn't have. Remember when you broke Mum's favourite vase? You owned up immediately, even knowing you'd be grounded forever.'

'I was a different person then.'

'No,' Lisette said firmly. 'You're still that person. You've just forgotten how to be brave.'

Her words struck something in him, a chord of truth he couldn't ignore. When had he become someone who hid from the truth? When had he stopped being the man Emily had fallen in love with?

'It's not too late,' Charlotte added softly. 'Emily loves you. She told you that herself.'

'She also said she couldn't trust me.'

'Then prove she can,' Rowena said

unexpectedly. 'I'll write down everything, tell her the whole truth about what happened.'

'No,' Julien said, resolve firming. 'No more messages or written explanations. I need to face her myself. Tell her everything, not just about that night, but about how scared I've been, how lost.' He stood, suddenly certain. 'I need to go to Sydney.'

'Now?' Charlotte asked, though she was already smiling.

'Now. Before I lose my nerve.' He turned to Rowena. 'I'm sorry for my part in this mess.'

'Me too,' she whispered. 'Now go fix things with Emily. And Julien? Tell her I'm sorry too.'

As he walked to his ute to head to the highway south, his sisters followed him out. The late afternoon sun painted everything in shades of gold, like the world was offering him one last chance to get things right.

'What if I go there and she still can't forgive me?' he asked, voicing his deepest fear.

'Then at least you'll know you were finally brave enough to try,' Lisette said, kissing his cheek.

'And Jules? Whatever happens, you're still our brother. We've got your back.'

Starting the engine, Julien felt something he hadn't experienced in months—hope. The trip to Sydney stretched ahead of him like a promise. He didn't know if Emily would forgive him, but he knew one thing: he was done hiding from the truth. It was time to be the man she'd fallen in love with again—the man who faced his mistakes head-on, who chose truth over comfort.

As his ute kicked up dust on the familiar road out of town, Julien made a silent promise. To Emily, to himself, to the person he used to be. No more lies, no more hiding. Whatever happened next, he would face it with honesty and courage.

Behind him, Rowena's voice called out Mason's name as she hurried along the road behind him. Everyone was finally choosing truth over fear. It was time he did the same.

Chapter 15

The Sydney coffee shop was nothing like the store in Duckinwilla Creek. No mismatched mugs, no handwritten specials board, no Lucy Lou popping in for her morning gossip. Everything here was sleek, modern, and efficient.

Emily stared at her perfectly made latte, watching the foam slowly dissolve into the coffee below, just like her dreams of small-town happiness, disappearing one sip at a time.

'Earth to Emily.' Kelly waved a hand in front of her face. 'You're a million miles away.'

'Sorry.' Emily forced a smile. 'Just thinking.'

'About him?' Kelly's voice was gentle. They'd been friends since their first teaching practicum, long before Duckinwilla Creek, before Julien, before everything fell apart.

'About everything.' Emily traced the rim of her cup. 'The job offer came through.'

'The one at Sydney Grammar?' Kelly's eyes widened. 'Em, that's amazing! Head of the

Preschool—it's exactly what you've always wanted.'

Was it? Emily wasn't sure anymore. Once, she'd dreamed of nothing but Sydney's prestigious private schools—polished corridors, faculty meetings, and curriculum development. But somewhere between morning coffees at the general store and sunset walks by the creek, those dreams had changed.

'I thought I knew what I wanted,' she said quietly. 'I thought I knew who I was.'

Kelly reached across the table, squeezing her hand. 'You're still you. One man's mistakes don't change that.'

'Don't they?' Emily pulled her hand back, wrapping it around her cooling coffee. 'Because I feel different. Like everything I thought I knew was just . . . I guess, not really what I wanted.'

'How long are you going to hide out here?' Kelly asked finally.

Emily traced a water ring on the table. 'I'm not hiding.'

'Really? Because from where I'm sitting, it looks a lot like hiding.'

Outside the café window, Sydney rushed past in a blur of school uniforms and morning traffic. So different from the lazy pace of Duckinwilla Creek, where a five-minute trip to the store could turn into an hour of catching up with neighbours. Julien would always have a fresh muffin waiting when she came down from the flat above each morning.

'I have a life here,' Emily said, but the words felt hollow. 'I always did.'

Kelly's expression softened. 'Having a life somewhere isn't the same as belonging there. And Em? You haven't belonged here since you left for Duckinwilla a month after meeting Julien.'

The truth of those words settled in Emily's chest like a stone. Before she could respond, her phone buzzed—another message from Charlotte. She'd been sending updates about the store, about town gossip, about everything except what Emily really wanted to know.

Was Julien okay? Did he still play that silly

"guess the flavour" game with the school kids who came in after classes? She'd caught him once, teaching a shy Year Seven student how to juggle with wrapped sweets, both of them laughing as the lollies scattered across the floor.

Emily pushed the thoughts away. It didn't matter anymore. She had the job offer. She had her Sydney life back. She had everything she'd thought she wanted before Duckinwilla Creek changed her dreams.

So why did it all feel so wrong? Why did the chime at the door of the coffee shop remind her of the store's door jangle?

Kelly was right. She was hiding. But not from Julien—from the truth about where she really belonged.

Chapter 16

Emily sat at her kitchen counter, staring at the coffee she'd just made but couldn't bring herself to drink. Julien's words from their phone call echoed in her head: 'I love you, Em.'

'I love you too,' she'd told him, and that was the heart of the problem. A movement caught her eye. Through her apartment window, she could see a sparrow pecking at the crumbs from her breakfast. They reminded her of mornings at the store when she'd watch them hop in the garden while she watered the herbs on the windowsill.

Tears spilled down her cheeks as memories flooded back—Julien teaching her to use the ancient cash register that sat beside the modern EFTPOS machine, his hands gentle over hers. The way he'd bring her coffee in their flat above the store, always remembering to add just a splash of milk. How he'd laugh at her city ways but defend her fiercely when anyone else did.

Her phone buzzed—another message from Charlotte.

He's different now. Really different. Give him a chance to prove it.

Before she could respond, a commotion in the street below drew her attention. A familiar ute had pulled up. She stood with her hand over her mouth and rushed to the bathroom, dragging out a face washer and scrubbing at her cheeks, and then ran a brush through her tangled hair, pulled off her T-shirt, and rummaged in her cupboard for a clean one. By the time the three tentative knocks sounded on her door, she had herself tidy but was shaking like a leaf.

She opened the door to find Julien standing there, dark circles under his eyes and his hair wild as though he'd been running his hands through it for hours.

'Hi,' he said softly.

Emily's hand tightened on the doorframe. Her eyes still felt raw from crying, and she knew he could see it despite her attempts to hide it. 'What are you doing here?'

'Being honest. Finally.' His voice cracked on the last word. 'Can I come in?'

She stepped back, letting him enter. The apartment felt smaller with him in it, full of memories she'd been trying to pack away like the boxes still stacked in the corner.

'I slept with Rowena,' he said without preamble, and Emily's breath caught. Not at the words—she'd already known, of course—but at the way he said them. No defensive edge, no careful denials. Just the plain truth, bare and raw.

'When?' she asked.

'That first month, when I came back from Sydney. We'd just started seeing each other, you and me. I hated leaving you, but I couldn't see a future for us. You with your dreams of a head teacher position and there I was, just taking over a small store in a country town.' He ran a hand through his hair. 'But that's not an excuse. It happened. Once. Before I realised—' he broke off, looking at her with desperate eyes.

'Before you realised what?'

'That you were the one for me. That what we had was real, not just some city girl passing through my life.' He took a step toward her, then stopped himself. 'But I lied to you when Rowena made her announcement at Charlotte's farewell, and I was too much of a coward to tell you the truth.'

Emily moved to the balcony, needing air. After a moment, he followed her out there. Below, Sydney buzzed with morning traffic, but up here, their world hung suspended.

Julien hesitated, then reached into his pocket. 'Actually, I have something for you.' He pulled out a small, weathered notebook. 'It's every lie I ever told you, written down. And next to each one is the truth. Even the small stuff.'

Emily took the notebook with trembling hands, thumbing through pages of Julien's familiar scrawl. Some entries made her smile despite herself:

Lie: *Told you I loved your city breakfast smoothies.*

Truth: *They tasted like lawn clippings, but your*

face lit up when you made them, so I drank every one.

Others made her heart ache:

Lie: *Said I was fine when Dad had his heart attack.*

Truth: *I was terrified of losing him, of letting everyone down, of not being strong enough.*

Lie: *Pretended the store was all I ever wanted.*

Truth: *Sometimes, I dream of travelling with you, seeing the world through your eyes before settling back home.*

She looked up at him, really looked at him, seeing not just the man who had lied to her but the one brave enough to bare all his truths.

'You wrote all of this?'

'Started the night you left, and I added more each time I stopped on the drive down. I couldn't sleep and kept thinking about every time I'd chosen the easy lie over the harder truth.' He ran a hand through his hair. 'There's some stuff in there I'm not proud of, Em. But it's all me. The good, the bad, the completely idiotic.'

Emily closed the notebook. 'And Rowena?'

'It meant nothing, and I regret it. But more importantly, I regret that I lied about it to you.' He took a deep breath. 'I was so scared of losing you that I did exactly that.'

Outside, the morning traffic hummed below them, and somewhere, a kookaburra laughed, the sound incongruous in the city setting like a piece of Duckinwilla Creek had followed them here, reminding Emily of home.

They sat on her balcony chairs, the morning sun warming their faces. Two cups of coffee grew cold between them as they talked, really talked, for the first time in what felt like forever.

'Tell me about everyone,' Emily said, drawing her knees up to her chest. 'I've missed them all so much.'

Julien smiled, and she could see the tension starting to ease from his shoulders. 'Well, you won't believe Amelia's hair—'

'Oh, I heard about that. Blue and orange, right?'

'Like a tropical bird had a fight with a paint tin,

Lisette says.' He laughed. 'But it suits her, somehow. It makes her look more . . . herself. She's talking about going to Japan to teach.'

'Japan?' Emily's eyebrows rose. 'How did your mother take that?'

'Surprisingly well, actually. Mum's been different since Dad's heart attack. Softer. Less worried about what people think. She's trying.' He twisted his coffee cup between his hands. 'She even defended Amelia when old Mrs Wilson made some comment about "proper young ladies" in the post office.'

Emily tried to imagine the proper Mrs Johnson doing that and couldn't quite manage it. 'And your dad?'

'Getting stronger every day. Makes these terrible jokes about having a "change of heart" about everything. You'd think he'd had a transplant.' His voice caught slightly. 'Those first few minutes in the hospital, Em, I've never been so scared. Made me realise what really matters in life.'

She reached out, touching his hand briefly. 'And

the store?'

'Charlotte and Greg have been amazing. They've modernised the inventory system, expanded the local produce section—' He paused. 'But I'm worried they might leave. I'd love them to stay and work with us.'

'Leave? Why?'

'Greg's parents own that big property out past Dunmora, and they're retiring to Elliot Heads. Greg's been talking about maybe taking it over, turning it into something special. Farm-to-table restaurant, maybe a bed and breakfast setup.'

'That sounds perfect for them,' Emily said softly.

'Yeah, it does.' Julien ran a hand through his hair. 'And that's what scares me. I always thought the store was my future, you know? The Johnson legacy. But watching Greg and Charlotte—they're building something real together. Something honest. I have a feeling that they've made a commitment and are waiting for the right time to tell the family. I sure haven't made it easy for them.'

Finally, she spoke. 'I have conditions. *If* I come back.'

'Anything.'

'First, no more lies. Not even small ones. If something's wrong, we talk about it.'

He nodded. 'Absolutely.'

'A fresh start,' she corrected. 'Second . . . I want us to build something real. Not just at the store, but in our life together. Something honest and strong, like what Charlotte and Greg have.'

'Deal,' he said softly, and something in his voice made her look up. Before she could move, he pulled her into his arms, holding her as though she might disappear if he let go.

'God, I've missed you,' he whispered into her hair. 'Missed your smile, your laugh, even the way you reorganise the store's shelves when you think no one's watching.'

His kiss, when it came, was gentle at first, tentative, as though they were both afraid of breaking this fragile new understanding between them. Then Julien's arms tightened around her waist, and Emily's hands slid into his hair, and suddenly, they were clinging to each other like they'd never let go.

'Was that a yes?' he asked, his voice rough. 'About coming home?'

Emily smiled, feeling truly whole for the first time in months. 'That was a yes to trying. To rebuild trust, to face whatever comes next. Together.'

The smile on Julien's face left no doubt—he loved her. At that moment, Emily knew they had begun to rebuild the trust between them, piece by piece, together.

Chapter 17

A month later

The morning light spilled across Duckinwilla Creek valley, warm and golden. Julien stood by the window of the General Store, watching the town come to life around him. His fingers traced the worn wooden counter, feeling the memories etched into every groove and scratch.

Outside, Duckinwilla Creek was waking up. Amelia, on her way to work, crossed the street with roses from Mum's garden for the tables. Old Mr Peters shuffled past with his dog. Lisette wiped down the tables outside, ready for the first customers, and Julien smiled as he watched his two younger sisters share a joke. Lucy Lou's salon buzzed with morning gossip, and a queue had already begun to form at Jerry's barber's shop.

And in the store that had seen many happy and sad days, Julien Johnson finally understood what it meant to be exactly where he belonged.

He took a deep breath. The aroma of coffee

brewing, polished wood, and the faintest hint of lavender—Emily's favourite—filled his lungs. He was home. And this time, he was staying. And with the woman he loved.

The creak of the stairs caught his attention, and moments later, Emily appeared, her work bag slung over her shoulder, already dressed for a day at the preschool. Her blonde hair was pulled back, a few wisps escaping around her face. Julien's arms opened wide, and she stepped into his embrace, rising on her tiptoes to press a soft kiss to his lips.

'Morning,' she murmured, pulling back with a smile. 'Busy day ahead?'

Julien chuckled. 'Not as busy as yours, I bet. But we've got that family dinner tonight. Mum wants it at the farm, but Grandmère—' he rolled his eyes dramatically '—insists on cooking. You know how she is.'

Emily's laugh was bright and musical. 'I love your family,' she said softly, her eyes meeting his.

A hint of vulnerability crept into his voice. 'As long as you love me too.'

'I do.' She stood on her toes and kissed him again. 'Now I have to go. We have a big day planned.'

'What's on today?'

'Well, while you're here playing gentleman grocer'—her grin was cheeky—'we have a nature walk with the preschoolers and a special project about local wildlife. Finger paints and stories about the creek, and maybe even a small garden to plant if we have time.'

'I think I'd rather be here,' he said, smiling at the excitement bubbling in her voice.

He still had to pinch himself to believe they were here, building a life together. In this town. A life that felt more solid and real than anything he'd ever known.

Emily took a ready-made salad roll and a bottle of water from the fridge and gathered her things, stealing one more kiss before heading out. The bell above the door chimed, a familiar sound that now marked the rhythm of their days together.

Julien watched her go, reflecting on his

happiness and satisfaction with life.

Julien Johnson finally understood what it meant to be exactly where he belonged.

Chapter 18

The farm

The rain fell softly on Mum's roses in the back garden, each drop catching the glow from the kitchen windows and turning to liquid gold. Oliver stood on the verandah, watching the water bead on the purple bougainvillea that had grown quickly up the new lattice frame Dad had built last week. The old Queenslander sat proudly, weatherboards gleaming pearl-grey in the dim evening light, surrounded by Dad's vegetable garden—a maze of herb beds and vegetables that somehow thrived together despite conventional wisdom. He'd taken over the vegetable garden as he recovered from his heart attack, much to Mum's relief.

Inside the kitchen, warmth and laughter filled the air and spilled through the window. Emily's voice carried through the open windows as she helped Grandmère with the cooking. Dad sat beside Mum at the kitchen table. Grandmère had insisted on taking over the farm kitchen for the night.

Emily insisted that Grandmère use the new recipe she'd brought back from Sydney for the chicken sauce. The way she and Julien had found their way back to each other still amazed Oliver; how they'd both needed that time apart to realise what they had together. Now they moved around each other with a new kind of confidence. Emily had taken up a part-time job at the preschool, and Julien was back running the General Store.

Guy was already at the table, absorbed in crop reports on his phone despite Grandmère's pointed looks. Some things would never change.

'Did you hear about Rowena and Mason?' Charlotte asked, reaching past Julien to steady a pot that teetered near the edge—still the fixer, even now that fewer things needed fixing.

'Moving to Longreach, aren't they?' Emily turned from the stove. 'Mason's got a position with a mining company.'

'Rowena's excited about it,' Julien added, his hand finding Emily's waist naturally as he reached past her for the bread knife. 'Says she's ready for a new adventure.'

'She'll have one of them when the baby's born,' Mum said.

'*Non, non,*' Grandmère waved them all away from the stove. 'Too many cooks. Sit, Charlotte, your fiancé is looking lonely.'

'Let them help, *Maman,*' Dad called from his armchair. 'Soon enough, we'll be missing Charlotte while she's living *la vie Parisienne* with Gregory.'

Oliver watched Charlotte's face soften at the mention of Paris. The tickets sat in an envelope on her fridge; he'd seen them last week when he'd dropped off some excess mangoes from the farm. A month away, but already her eyes got dreamy whenever France came up.

'It's just a holiday,' Greg said from his spot at the table, but his smile was knowing. Oliver wondered if they'd decided to stay there longer than they were letting on. He pushed away a pang of envy at their certainty, their easy connection. He knew they had plans to settle eventually at Greg's parents' farm.

'A holiday that was too long in coming, but we all appreciated you helping out, didn't we, Hugo?' Mum said as she picked up a rose petal that had fallen from the vase in the middle of the table. She looked better these days—the shadows under her eyes had faded, and to everyone's surprise, she'd taken up painting. Right now, there was a smudge of blue paint behind her ear that no one had been game to mention; they still tiptoed around her.

Amelia bounced in from the bathroom, her hair now a more subdued red instead of the shocking blue and orange it had been a couple of months ago. 'I still can't believe Rowena's going to be so far away. Who's going to run the book club now?'

'Some of us have actual work to do,' Guy muttered, finally looking up from his phone.

'Unlike Mason, who's clearly just going there for a holiday,' Emily teased, and everyone laughed at Guy's embarrassed flush.

'Speaking of work,' Lisette had appeared beside Oliver on the verandah, two glasses of wine in hand. She offered him one. 'You missed all the excitement at the store last week. Julien brought in Emily's whole class of kindergarteners for a tour.'

Oliver accepted the wine, watching through the window as Julien dramatically re-enacted something for the table, Emily shaking her head but laughing. 'How did that go?'

'Chaos. Complete chaos. But the good kind.' Lisette smiled—actually smiled, without the edge that had been there for the past few years. It looked like she had finally moved on from the drama that had seen her and Charlotte at odds for a long time. 'One little girl asked Emily if she was a princess because she married the man from the lolly shop.'

Oliver choked on his wine. Inside, Julien was now helping Emily serve the *coq au vin*, their movements synchronised like they'd never been apart. It was strange to think how, just months ago, he'd been camped in Sydney, desperate to win her back. Now they looked so . . . settled.

'It's different when you find the right person,' Lisette said quietly as if reading his thoughts. 'Look at them. Look at Charlotte and Greg. Even Rowena and Mason—moving across the state for love and adventure.' She nudged his shoulder. 'You look like you're watching everyone else live while you're stuck in pause.'

'I don't—'

'It's okay.' Her smile was gentle. 'We all get stuck sometimes. Look at me. I nearly ruined everything because I was too proud to admit I was jealous of how easy everyone else made it look.'

Inside, Grandmère was shooing everyone to their seats as Emily served up. Dad was already at the head of the dining room table, looking tired but happy, his colour better than it had been in months.

'Come on, time to join the rabble,' Lisette said. 'Unless you want Grandmère to come and fetch us herself.'

Oliver followed her inside, the warmth wrapping around him as it always did. The old dining room looked the same: family photos covering the walls, the ancient sideboard groaning with plates and serving dishes, the chandelier that Papa had restored casting a soft light over everything. But something had shifted in the atmosphere over the past months. The tension that had crackled through recent family dinners had eased, replaced by something happier.

'Oliver, *mon petit*,' Grandmère commanded from her seat beside Papa, 'help me with this bread.'

He moved automatically to slice the still-warm baguettes, ending up between Amelia and Lisette, across from Emily and Julien, who were sharing some private joke. Charlotte and Greg sat nearby, heads bent together over what looked like a Paris map, while Guy finally put his phone away as Papa said grace.

'I can't believe you're leaving next week, Charlie,' Amelia said as they passed dishes around. 'Everyone's having adventures except me.'

'Our preschool isn't adventurous enough for you?' Emily asked, spooning out vegetables. 'Trust me, thirty five-year-olds is all the adventure anyone needs.'

'Better than Japan,' Mum said, and everyone tactfully ignored Amelia's eye roll.

The conversation flowed easily as they ate; Amelia talked about her upcoming traineeship and her TAFE course, Charlotte and Greg discussed their itinerary, and Emily described her students' reaction to seeing where all the lollies came from when Julien had let the class come to the store. Even Guy emerged from his agricultural reverie to debate the merits of different mango varieties with Dad.

'Mason's working in the mines, but he reckons there are good farming opportunities further north,' Guy mentioned. 'Different crops, obviously, but the principles are the same.'

'You're not thinking of following them to Longreach, are you?' Charlotte asked sharply.

Guy pulled a face. 'Sugar cane doesn't grow at Longreach.'

'Someone's got to stay and look after the family farm,' Oliver found himself saying. 'Besides, who else would sell mangoes at the markets?'

The table went quiet for a moment before erupting in gentle laughter and knowing looks.

'The markets?' Emily leaned forward,

interested. 'Where the pretty girl chatted you up last weekend? Amelia mentioned her.'

Heat crept up Oliver's neck. 'No, she wasn't. She was just asking about the fruit.'

'She was flirting with you,' Amelia insisted. 'And you? You just talked about fruit varieties for ten minutes.'

Outside, the rain fell harder, drumming on the tin roof. The garden would be drinking it in, Mum's roses lifting their heads to the water. Oliver thought about that girl: the way her eyes had crinkled when she smiled, how her fingers had lingered over the fruit selection. Maybe Amelia was right. Maybe he had missed something, too worried about being boring to notice someone might find him interesting. He hadn't even asked her name.

'Oliver will help me with dessert,' Grandmère announced, rising from the table. It wasn't a request.

In the kitchen, she handed him plates while she dished up her famous *crème brûlée*. 'You know what your problem is, *mon cher*?'

'I'm sure you'll tell me, Grandmère.'

'You think too much.' She tapped his forehead with a floury finger. 'Up here, always watching, always waiting. Look at your brother with that phone, your sister with her Japan dreams. Sometimes, the ones who rush around miss what's right in front of them. But you, you see everything except yourself.'

Oliver thought about the girl at the market, about the way she'd written her phone number on the back of her receipt before leaving it carefully on his table. 'I wouldn't know where to start.'

'Did Julien know? Did Greg?' Grandmère's eyes twinkled. 'Love isn't about knowing; it's about trying. About being brave enough to look foolish sometimes.'

Back at the table, the conversation had turned to Emily and Julien's engagement party. 'We should host it at the store,' Lisette was saying. 'Like we did for Charlotte and Greg's engagement. That was the best party.'

Everyone spoke at once. 'I don't want to have our party where we work all day,' Julien protested.

'Do you, Em?'

'I'm happy wherever we have it,' she said, looking down at the shiny engagement ring on her left hand.

'As long as Guy puts his phone away that night,' Amelia teased. 'I'm just saying if you spent as much time talking to actual women as you give to your spreadsheets . . . you might meet someone new. Some of your friends are coming from Sydney, aren't they, Emily?'

'Some of us have a business to run,' Guy protested. 'I don't think about parties.'

'The farm won't collapse if you look away from your phone for five minutes,' Dad said mildly. 'Trust me, I checked.'

Oliver set down the dessert plates, something heavy settling in his chest. They were right—all of them. About Guy's phone, his tendency to overthink, the way life could pass you by if you let it.

'I'm going to the markets again next weekend,' he said suddenly, surprising himself. 'To sell the last of the mangoes.'

The conversation paused, and he felt everyone trying not to look too interested.

'Really?' Amelia's grin was broad. 'Any particular reason?'

Oliver spooned up some *crème brûlée*, fighting a smile. 'The mangoes won't sell themselves.'

'No,' Emily said softly, exchanging a knowing look with Julien. 'Sometimes, they need a little help.'

The rain drummed on, but inside the dining room at the farm, surrounded by the warm chaos of his family, Oliver felt something shift. A decision, maybe. Or just a willingness to step into the dance, as Grandmère had said.

He looked around the table—at Charlotte and Greg planning their adventure, Amelia practising Japanese on her napkin, Emily and Julien sharing private smiles, Lisette relaxed and laughing, and Guy finally setting down his phone to really join in. At Mum and Dad, together and healing, and Grandmère presiding over it all with knowing eyes.

Papa sitting back, content, observing his family.

Maybe being quiet didn't mean being stuck. Maybe it just meant he noticed things others missed—like the way the girl's fingers had lingered on the mangoes or how her phone number was still burning a hole in his wallet.

Tomorrow, he decided, he would call. After all, Julien and Charlotte had taken a chance on love. Maybe it was finally his turn.

Coming in April

Book 3: Wishes and Whispers

Oliver Johnson's life revolves around dawn-to-dusk work on his family's cane farm - until his well-meaning sister Amelia creates his online dating profile. Between awkward video chats, mistaken identities, and disastrous first dates, Oliver begins to wonder if true love is worth all this trouble. But when an intriguing message appears in his inbox, he discovers that finding romance might be sweeter than he expected... if he can just stop accidentally setting things on fire first. A charming romantic comedy about love, family meddling, and finding connection in the digital age.

eBook:

https://books2read.com/u/bakqv2

Print:

https://annieseatonstore.ecwid.com/Wishes-and-Whispers-Pre-order-April-p722599746

Also by Annie Seaton

Daughters of the Darling

From Across the Sea

Over the River

By the Billabong (2025)

A Bec Whitfield Mystery

Bowen River

Shadows on the Shore (June 2025)

Duckinwilla Days (2025)

Coming Home

Secrets and Surprises

Wishes and Whispers

New Beginnings

Home to the Outback *(2025)*

Lucy

Angie

Jemima

Isabella

Porter Sisters Series

Kakadu Sunset

Daintree

Diamond Sky

Hidden Valley

Larapinta

Kakadu Dawn

Others

Whitsunday Dawn

Undara

Osprey Reef

East of Alice

One Summer in Tuscany

Four Seasons Short and Sweet

Follow the Sun

Ten Days in Paradise

Deadly Secrets

Adventures in Time

Silver Valley Witch

The Emerald Necklace

A Clever Christmas

Christmas with the Boss

Her Christmas Star

The Emerald Necklace

The Augathella Girls Series

Outback Roads

Outback Sky

Outback Escape

Outback Wind

Outback Dawn

Outback Moonlight

Outback Dust

Outback Hope

Boxed Sets

Augathella Girls 1-4

Augathella Girls 5-8

Augathella Short and Sweet Series

An Augathella Surprise

An Augathella Baby

An Augathella Spring

An Augathella Christmas

An Augathella Wedding

An Augathella Easter

An Augathella Masquerade Ball

Boxed Set

Augathella Short and Sweet 1-3

Sunshine Coast Series

Waiting for Ana

The Trouble with Jack

Healing His Heart

Sunshine Coast Boxed Set

The Richards Brothers Series

The Trouble with Paradise

Marry in Haste

Outback Sunrise

Richards Brothers Boxed Set

Bondi Beach Love Series

Beach House

Beach Music

Beach Walk

Beach Dreams

The House on the Hill Boxed Set

Second Chance Bay Series

Her Outback Playboy

Her Outback Protector

Her Outback Haven

Her Outback Paradise

Boxed Set

The McDougalls of Second Chance Bay Boxed Set

Love Across Time Series

Come Back to Me

Follow Me

Finding Home

The Threads that Bind

Boxed Set

Love Across Time 1-4

Bindarra Creek

Worth the Wait

Full Circle

Secrets of River Cottage

A Clever Christmas

A Place to Belong

About the Author

Annie lives in Australia, on the beautiful north coast of New South Wales. She sits in her writing chair and looks out over the tranquil Pacific Ocean.

She writes contemporary romance and loves telling stories that always have a happily ever after.

She lives with her very own hero of many years and they share their home with Barney, the rag doll puss, who hides when the four grandchildren come to visit.

Stay up to date with her latest releases at her website: **http://www.annieseaton.net**

If you would like to stay up to date with Annie's releases, subscribe to her newsletter here: http://www.annieseaton.net

9 781764 001601